LITTLE SQUIRE JIM

LITTLE SQUIRE JIM

ROBERT K. MARSHALL

A Knight ther was, and that a worthy man,
That fro the tyme that he first bigan
To ryden out, he loved chivalrye . . .

With him ther was his sone, a yong Squyer,
A lovyere, and a lusty bacheler. . . .

—From Chaucer's Prologue to *The Canterbury Tales*

DUELL, SLOAN AND PEARCE · NEW YORK

Copyright, 1949, by

ROBERT K. MARSHALL

*All rights reserved, including
the right to reproduce this book
or portions thereof in any form.*

First Edition

Printed in the United States of America

C. 2

TO KATHRYN

9112- 22

CONTENTS

"There is a strangeness, a wonderful strangeness, about the South," said Benjamin T.

"You mean Kentucky?" I smiled, for I knew he was from Kentucky.

"Anyhow, Kentucky," he answered.

"But what about North Carolina and Louisiana and Virginia?"

"Oh, Virginia is Virginia, as any good Virginian has known for a long time. And a good Louisianian probably never thought of North Carolina as part of the South. That's part of the wonderful strangeness."

LITTLE SQUIRE JIM

PROLOGUE

The streets of Tateboro on that August Saturday were nearly deserted. Across from the Courthouse three men stood around a massive bay stallion tethered under an oak tree in front of Old Judge Tate's house. The stallion was a magnificent animal, with broad shoulders and a high head, and mane a deep red. Impatiently it scraped the pavement with its front hoof and tossed its head.

When the clock near the pointed roof above the white

13

columns of the Courthouse showed one minute before eleven-thirty, a man on the edge of a crowd on the Courthouse steps suddenly raised his hand, in the way of a signal. At his sign one of the men about the stallion under the tree loosened the strap from around the trunk. The stallion reared in a sudden violent arc, pawing the air with its forelegs, and made the sun slide down its sides and haunches in rippling waves of bright copper.

"Tell the Little Squire," the man at the strap shouted, "that he's rearin to fly."

Over the wide streets of Tateboro the branches of maple and oak trees tangled their branches and leaves, and behind these trees, on lawns carelessly kept, sat simple pre-Civil War homes, their doorways and windows weathered and in need of paint, and now and then a more pretentious house, like the Old Judge Tate house, with its tall white columns in front rising to a high roof, giving to the porch and facade an imposing classic beauty. Among these pre-Civil War homes sat later Victorian structures, with porches and cornices frilled with jigsaw lace, and between these Victorian homes an occasional bungalow or Dutch Colonial to make the casual visitor to Tateboro certain that he was still in a modern day.

But whatever the streets or homes of Tateboro might suggest, the center of life and activity of Tate County was about the Courthouse that sat so benignly on its tree-shaded knoll in the middle of the Square. The Courthouse was a long, rectangular building of faded pink brick with

14

six massive Doric columns in front, and on court days, about the curbs and lawn, trucks and cars discolored with red clay from the back hills shared space with mule-drawn wagons smelling of corn or hay or tobacco.

In its time Tateboro Courthouse had seen many a tempestuous court-trial. It was the scene, back in the 1790's, of the first legal battles of Andrew Jackson, young and fresh from his student days in Salisbury less than sixty miles away, before he turned west through the mountains into Tennessee. The Courthouse has records of these trials, but in Tateboro there are also more personal mementos of his days there—a handleless cup and saucer from which Jackson once drank his coffee mixed with whiskey, still kept in the lobby of Tateboro Inn across the street from the Courthouse, and a copy of Bacon's *Essays,* in the library of Tate house, from which Jackson tore a page to write an angry challenge to an opponent who outsmarted him on a legal point. Old Judge Tate in his day never missed an opportunity to show the book, and he would recount the details of the duel with such enthusiasm and vividness of detail that soon it was he, and not his father, who was the active participant in the duel. And after him his son, William, had a tendency to re-fight the duel in such a way that the listener wouldn't know whether it was William or his grandfather who had been the hero. A confusing of fact and time and family not confined to the Tates. In the South, at any rate.

Although the records of the Courthouse are less imaginative than the Tates' dueling exploits, they show that in the 1840's, about the time the white columns were added to the portico, the Courthouse witnessed violent scenes over

15

slave ownerships; and, in the 1870's, angry battles over unpaid taxes and carpetbag ownership claims. And, as late as 1910, its walls were shaken by pistol shots and the anger of the clannish Llewellens from Low Gap, who decided, as the trial against them was drawing to an end, that they didn't like the look on the faces of the jury.

But not until Little Squire Jim Boyden was drawn into Tateboro Courthouse had a Boyden from Little Stepper Valley ever been inside its walls, not even to pay taxes, since the time Big Jim Boyden, Little Squire Jim's father, sued Julia Gwynn—Mrs. Joseph Huger Gwynn—over the terms of the Paget will, and lost.

Julia Gwynn was half-sister to Big Jim's wife, Amelia Paget Boyden, and therefore Little Squire Jim's half-aunt. She drew her dividends from Anders Mill, on the outskirts of Tateboro, in the modern way, but she had a sign posted outside the gates that opened into the cedar-lined drive that wound up the hill to Gwynn Place, ten miles below Tateboro: 'No motor vehicles allowed within these portals.' She also kept a 'barouche landau' with coat of arms on the door brightly gilded, a coachman in silk top-hat on the box, and when she drove into Tateboro, even as late as the 'twenties, at the first sound of her horses' hoofs on the pavement far down the street the children would send up a cry, "Old Lady Gwynn's wild-ridin,'" as children in Tateboro had done for over thirty years, and rush to the street to watch her whirl by. She was a kind of elegant fantasy in their lives. To their elders, however, Mrs. Gwynn was a tragic figure whose domestic problem was not to be discussed before children, though enough words were dropped so that

16

the children sometimes asked, "When Old Lady Gwynn shoots her husband, can we go to the court-trial too?" It was like that for a long time in Tateboro. But whatever was said and thought—and there was a great deal said and thought about Mrs. Gwynn in Tateboro over thirty years— it was still a mark of social distinction if her barouche landau were seen waiting in front of anyone's house.

But Little Squire Jim had only blood relationship with Mrs. Gwynn. No more. He was born and lived back in the mountains northwest of Tateboro, near Crocketts Cove, where good roads had not penetrated; where trees and paths climbed up to a man's doorstep—if he lived where Thag Totten did, up Sleeping Father Mountain, close to Hanging Rock; where a cloud might sit on a man's front step and mist his windows before slipping quietly out over the yard, leaving far below a great blue valley; or where, down in the hollows and bottomlands—if he lived where Annie Umbarger did—the January snows might fall on violets in bloom, and the rhododendron and laurel were thick along the paths; and where time was measured by what a man's father could recollect of what his grandfather had heard *his* grandfather say.

The people who lived up near Crocketts Cove were out of those people who sailed in the 1600's from the old country, landed on the sandbars of North Carolina, and in time trekked from the coast over the low country and plains to the foothills, and then into the security and isolation of the mountains, bringing with them the ways and customs of the old country, and holding on to these customs through years and years and years—old customs of devotions to funerals, religious and political antagonisms, dignity of

17

personal rights, resentment to intrusion, and a feeling for the 'fitness' of things. Their speech still held rhythms of Chaucer, and of Elizabethan England, and echoes of Celtic lore; the woes of Barby Allen and the tragic jealousy of the 'Twa Sisters' over one man were sung to them in their cradles.

Loyalties ran deep with them, too. Being a Democrat or a Republican, a Protestant or a Catholic, made a difference, just as it had made a difference to their forebears whether a man was a Royalist or a Parliamentarian. It was in the blood. It made a difference in the 'twenties when the Democrats ran Catholic Al Smith for President. Many a Democrat from Crocketts Cove in anger scratched the name of Al Smith and wrote in the name of Andrew Jackson, just to keep the record clear and the heart clean. And out of these people Little Squire Jim Boyden came.

The Boydens had lived in Little Stepper Valley, near Crocketts Cove, since anyone about the Cove could possibly imagine—red-haired all of them and handsome, and possessing a dignity and bearing that came from owning land that had come into their name by King Charles's grant. The earlier Boydens found outlet in the Virginia lands across the border; but the Old Squire and, after him, Big Squire, Little Squire Jim's father, preferred a more secluded life in Little Stepper Valley on the North Carolina side. And in time the Boydens became rights of possession of the Cove folk, and in his day the sight of Big Jim Boyden riding out of the Valley on his fierce black horse and up into a man's yard was an act of warm generosity, to be cherished and talked about. "Heared the Big Squire stopped by fer a visit tother day. Git him to speak of the election, or of Old Lady Gwynn?" "No, jest passed the time of day." "Well, it'd pleasure me ef he'd drop by fer a spell in my yard and cuss the Old Lady before he gits killed."

They loved to hear the Big Squire grow profane about his wife's half-sister, Mrs. Gwynn. There was music in the violence of his profanity, like the winds over the valleys. And they spoke of his getting killed as matter-of-factly as they walked under Hanging Rock that beetled above Dave Crockett's mill.

So it was that when the Little Squire was drawn into court the Cove folk walked or rode, as each could, into Tateboro.

Near sundown those tending the stallion brought water and hay to feed it, and as the shadows along the street grew into a twilight and the street lights began to flicker on, the men about the stallion whispered to each other and pointed toward the jail window, high and barred, at the far side of the Courthouse. The stallion, too, pointed its ears toward the window and whinnied.

The next morning the stallion was still there. When the men had fed it and the guard had changed, they curried the horse's coat into a sleek redness, combed its mane carefully, and when the children going to Sunday school passed, and later their parents on the way to church, they stopped, fascinated by the wildness of the animal, the muscular beauty of its shoulders, and the anger in its restive eyes.

At one o'clock the jury had dinner sent in on a tray.

At about two-thirty, far down the street, the men around

19

the stallion heard the grind of carriage wheels. Til Umbarger got out into the street to see the better. "Old Lady Gwynn's comin to help out the Little Squire," he cried. "She's comin to help out the Little Squire."

But Julia Gwynn's carriage only swept by them, turned the corner at the Square, and disappeared down Hill Street. Half an hour later it came rattling by again, swerving wide to miss them, and went on down Main Street, and the men could only turn and stare helplessly at each other, hearing the clatter and grinding wheels losing themselves far down the street and out of sight.

The next morning, a little before eight o'clock, Lucy McVay came up Hill Street from Anderstown. She waved to the men around the stallion and shouted in a gusty voice: "I'm gitten there early to git a seat. I haven't lived all my born days to miss what the Little Squire's gonna do when the law sets out to tech him. And I'll keep a seat beside me fer you, Til Umbarger, ef it's to yore likin."

A half-hour later a girl of eighteen or nineteen, her green high-heeled snakeskin shoes and pocketbook matching, also turned the corner from Hill Street looking to the Square. She was an unusually pretty girl; her bright auburn hair was plaited in braids about the crown of her head. When she saw the men near the horse she gasped and ran toward them. The stallion, too, seeing her coming, nickered and scraped the street with its front hoof, pointing its ears toward her.

"Oh," she cried, putting up her hand, "I believe he remembers me." The stallion tossed its head at her touch.

"Hit's a sign," one of the men near her burst out. "He's not let anybody tech him like that since Little Squire's been

20

up there," and he gestured toward the high window in the corner of the jail.

The girl's hand on the stallion trembled, and the man leaned over her shoulder and whispered so low that no one else could hear him, "Tell the Little Squire we're keepin him untied and standin ready, so he ken git right on him and fly off to the mountains, when he calls."

She made no answer, and kept her face away. In a moment, without turning, she hurried across the street to the jail.

The men watched her until she had disappeared. Finally the one who had whispered to her said abruptly: "Lucy McVay's keepin a seat fer me in the court room, and I'm goin over and git in before I caint git in. Keep the strop loose, like we agreed."

Now, except for the two men by the red horse and the people crowding up the steps of the Courthouse, trying to get inside, the Square was deserted. Silence came over the streets, over the lawn, over the edges of the crowd and over the watchmen in front of Tate house.

Ten minutes passed. Then a man called out, "The jury's in, and they've sent fer the Little Squire."

Ten more minutes passed. Twenty minutes. Then a feeling passed out of the Courthouse, and the edges of the crowd outside became tense. Suddenly from within came a roar. And rising above this a cry of a woman's voice, loud and ecstatic: "Hit's the Big Squire turnin in his grave and shakin the mountains. Hit's the Big Squire turnin in his grave!"

"Unloose the strop," one of the watchmen cried; "hit's Lucy McVay singin out."

21

The stallion began to tremble, its neck arching, its nostrils distending, and its eyes lighting. The man at the strap fumbled with the knot, and then through the trees came Little Jim's voice itself, ringing across the knoll, cutting through the turmoil: "Take your hands off me. Take your hands off me."

At the sound of that call the stallion reared in a convulsive wheel, its forelegs in the air, and sent forth an answering call, strident and wild. Breaking the strap, tearing itself from the men, with hoofs pounding the street it gained momentum to leap up the terrace of the Courthouse lawn, and with heavy thud of hoofs crossed the lawn and clattered up the marble steps.

From across the street came the yell: "Git out of his way! Caint you see he's ridin to the cry of Little Squire Jim!"

L U C Y M<small>c</small> V A Y

The road from Tateboro to Crocketts Cove curves through the foothills, twists up the side of Sleeping Father Mountain, and then drops down along Blue Snake Creek past Dave Crockett's mill and goes on between Sleeping Father Mountain and Big Stepper Mountain into Virginia; and high above Dave Crockett's mill, a half-mile or more, is Old Hanging Rock, a monster cliff of stone, broken from Sleeping Father Mountain in some prehistoric upheaval and left resting on a thin base. At times wisps of clouds rest upon it. The crevice

23

between it and Sleeping Father Mountain—which looks so narrow from far below—is wide enough for high winds to pass through, sending forth a wail that sets the hearts of the Cove folk to beating. "Sounds like the yellin of the Old Squire the night he rode the lightnin to his grave," they whisper.

If anyone climbs the sides of Sleeping Father Mountain and crawls to the cliff edge, he will find that the crevice is wide, too wide for any mortal man to jump. Across this fissure, however, the Rock is a broad, flat crown of a stone head that frowns down upon Blue Snake Creek, a thin wire in the sun far below, and upon the small dark squares of Dave Crockett's mill and house. To the south, on the side of Sleeping Father Mountain, lie Thag Totten's lands, where house and stables make brown patches in the red-and-green tilled fields; and farther on, hidden behind a sharp ridge and down in a hollow, along Reams Creek, is Annie Umbarger's cabin.

To the east, in a blue haze, lies Little Stepper Valley, cradled between Big Stepper and Little Stepper Mountains. The Valley is long and narrow, and wild with virgin growth, impenetrable and almost unknown to anyone living about the Cove, except the oldest of living men; for it is almost forty years since the Old Squire's burial, and nearly fifteen years since Big Jim Boyden took his bride, Amelia Paget, into the Valley. And since that time no one except Lucy McVay has known with surety what lies in there.

Lucy McVay was Annie Umbarger's sister, and when the two were younger—before Lucy came down from Crocketts

Cove to be midwife in Henry Anders' mill village—she and Annie used to go about the mountains singing ballads, with a zither of their own making on their knees. For the asking they would sing countless ballads from the old country and a hundred of their own making. But singing ballads was not a livelihood, and Lucy practiced midwifery, as her mother and grandmother before her had done, and Sister Annie practiced herb-cures. When Annie married Til Umbarger things did not continue so harmoniously with the two sisters. Some said it was Lucy's disappointment that Annie did not return the attentions of Thag Totten, who with his two brothers owned half the side of Sleeping Father Mountain right up to Hanging Rock and grew more corn than they ever took to Dave Crockett's grist mill. Others, perhaps more discerning, said that Lucy held more than passing affection for Til, and that all was not too easy with the three of them in one house. At any rate, soon after the still-birth of Annie's only child, a son, Lucy wandered down from Crocketts Cove to be the granny-woman in Anderstown.

In time she grew into a stout, robust woman with gray-streaked hair, an apronstring always tight around the middle of her gray homespun dress. She led a busy life. She was in constant demand as a midwife and she was funeral assistant besides; she was as skillful at a laying-out as she was at a birthing, and just as zestful, for Lucy was a boisterous woman. Many a wake was enlivened by her ballads and her gusty laughter. And as if this were not enough to cover her loneliness at being away from the hills of Crocketts Cove and from Sister Annie, she did a lively business in corn whiskey—for the heart and spirit, she maintained, getting

25

it twice a year from some mysterious source back in the mountains, in a load of pumpkins, some said.

But of all Lucy McVay's distinctions, she cherished the fact that she had been in Little Stepper Valley the night Little Squire Jim was born. "Yes, sir," she would chant, "I were there fer the first yelp, and his maw a-tearin at the bridle and cryin pope-words like any Christian woman, and the Big Squire walkin the floor and wantin to know ef it were man or animal." And her eyes would grow bright, and her sallow cheeks would begin to take on a glow. "And look what the Big Squire give me," she would cry, reaching into her bosom and bringing out a little bag tied with a string. From it she would take his gift and rub it to a glow with thumb and forefinger. "And I'm savin it to go to Little Squire's buryin when he gits killed fer a Boyden man."

It was a stormy night in late October when the leaves were brown, she would tell, when the lightning was sitting on Old Hanging Rock in ropes and curls and beads of light, and far over the mountain the thunder was rolling and arguing and shaking the clouds, that she and Sister Annie were sitting—just the two of them—in the cabin along Reams Creek. The fire on the hearth flared up fitfully, lighting the room, the chests, the handmade chairs and four-poster bed with its trundle underneath, and the herbs and roots hanging from the rafters and along the mantel. An empty cradle was in the far corner.

Sister Annie, small, dwarfish, with sharp, bright eyes and fingers small and birdlike, rocked nervously in her chair, her little feet hardly touching the floor. As a fresh gust of

26

rain hit the logs outside, she glanced uneasily toward the cradle. Lucy saw the glance and murmured:

"Hit don't do no good to grieve, Annie."

"I know, I know," Annie answered, her fingers working more rapidly with the herbs.

"Ef Til had've . . ."

"Hit were not Til's fault that it were still-born," Annie answered, bending over her herbs more closely.

A slash of rain hit the window. "Til had no right to be up to Hangin Rock layin traps," Lucy said, "and hit blowin to drown a man."

"Til's a man to know his way in the dark, and hit a-rainin and thunderin," Annie answered defensively, still bending over her dried leaves.

Lucy reached down beside her chair to lift up a box of new herbs to tie into little sacks. "I sometimes git to thinkin how it'd a-been ef you'd a-welcomed Thag Totten," she murmured.

"Til Umbarger were fer me, and I were fer him," Annie answered, rocking more rapidly.

A strained silence fell between them. Annie got up and put a new log on the fire. The flames sprang, letting sparks fall on the hearth. She came back to her chair and, reaching over, gathered up her trays of powdered leaves. As she did so, from outside, along the path that led up to the steps, she heard the sound of metal shoe against a stone, and then a pounding on the door with the butt of a riding crop. "Hullo in there."

"That's not Til," Annie said.

"Then open the door and ask his name," Lucy answered.

Annie hastily put her herbs on a chest and went to the

27

door. She slid back the bar and peered out through the narrow opening. "Oh," she gasped, "hit's the Big Squire, and him ridin up in a body's yard like a mortal man." She swung the door wide.

Outside, Big Jim Boyden sat on his horse. He was a handsome man, like all the Boyden men, with a great muscular rhythm in his every movement. His shoulders were broad and powerful, his head large, with a proud thrust of the chin. His eyes were blue under his heavy brows and his hair red enough, the Cove folk maintained, to set the sun on fire; and that night, as he sat outside the door on his black horse, himself muffled in a heavy dark coat, collar turned high, its length down over his boots and spurs, he seemed more powerful and commanding than ever.

"Is Lucy McVay ready to go?" he asked, his eyes sweeping the inside of the cabin.

"To go?" Lucy gasped.

"For a birthin, and there's never a minute to say no," he went on, pulling the restive Blackfire back against the cabin steps.

"You mean," Lucy stammered, "you want old Lucy to come into Little Stepper Valley to—"

"The mare's cryin to God-amercy and needin the help of Lucy McVay."

"But . . ."

"Get your tools," he roared, his blue eyes turning dark in impatience.

Lucy spun about the room. "Git me my box, Annie," she said, her voice shaking and trembling, "fer the leaves and the roots. And I'll git my satchel and things." Quickly she opened a chest and took from it a leather pouch, cumber-

28

some and heavy to her lift, the long handle of an axe sticking from its flap. She set it out into the room. Then, throwing a heavy coat over her shoulders and a thick black shawl over her head, she took the box Annie handed her and lifted the satchel, ready to go. Through the door, Blackfire pawed the turf and showed his teeth.

"The satchel up front, and you up behind," the Big Squire ordered, pulling his horse around to the step again.

Lucy drew back. "A-holdin onto you on that black hoss, and ridin into the Valley on a night like this?"

"Onto the horse, woman," he cried, reaching over for the satchel. "The mare deliverin, and you cryin words of delay!"

"Hit's the Big Squire askin," Annie cried, urging Lucy forward.

Annie handed the satchel up to the Squire, who swung it onto the saddle point. But Lucy still held back in terror.

"Onto the horse, woman," he roared again.

"But . . ."

Annie pushed her sister toward the door. "Aint it the Big Squire askin?" she cried.

Lucy, unable to do otherwise, found herself climbing up behind with Annie's fumbling assistance, clutching at the heavy coat in terror. The Squire dug spurs, and they sprang into the night with rattle of stones and metal. What way they took Lucy McVay could never tell. She only knew that they did not take the road past Crockett's mill that led toward the boulders marking the entrance to Little Stepper Valley. In the darkness and rain she could recognize nothing. She could only cling to the Big Squire while the black horse tore through trees, jumping high streams, up steep,

29

precipitous inclines, over a high rocky shoulder against the mountain, wet limbs tearing at their coats. The easy rhythm of the galloping horse on the occasional open stretches was the only sure thing she knew. At times it seemed they rode into blinding flashes of lightning, flaming about them, then to drop suddenly down with thunder roaring close behind them. Finally they came to more even ground, and the horse leveled out, breathing hard, but still pounding on. Suddenly in a flash of lightning Little Stepper House loomed up in front of them, dark and massive.

The Big Squire pulled around to the back. Yellow light shone through the windows of a back wing. An old Negro man and a young Negro boy came out of the shadows, one catching the bridle, the other assisting Lucy to the ground. The Big Squire led the way into the kitchen. A log was burning in the stone fireplace, with kitchen kettles and irons over it. A large hutch table littered with utensils seemed to fill the dim room. In the far corner, under a crucifix, a candle flickered in a rose cup. Lucy caught her breath in dismay. But before she could gather herself to so much as cover her eyes at the sight of it, an old Negro woman, her head wrapped in a dingy gray cloth, came to help her remove her coat and shawl.

"She's sweatin and cryin to de Mary-woman," she said to the Squire.

Without taking off his own coat the Big Squire led the way through the kitchen into a hallway that turned slightly in its passage. From a room at the end came a pleading cry, "Jim, Jim, is that you?" He threw open a heavy door. "In there, woman."

Lucy went in. It was a large, dim bedroom, with high

30

ceiling, and its corners far away in shadows. A fire from the open hearth etched out great carved pieces of furniture. In a high tester-bed, its canopy dusty and fringed with dull gold tassels, Amelia Boyden lay, her eyes feverish in spasms of agony, her lips muttering broken prayers to the Holy Mother, and crying to her husband, who stood unanswering in the doorway. A candle burned before a crucifix on a massive chest near the bed.

At the sight of the candle Lucy tried to turn back. "Hit's against my cures," she cried, terror in her eyes.

"They bring peace to the house," the Big Squire scowled, barring the door. "Close your eyes."

"And she's a woman from a fer land," she cried.

"She's a Paget, and sister to the woman of Gwynn's Place, just over the mountain." There was resentment in his voice, but there was pride too.

"A candle-lightin woman's from a fer land to me," Lucy insisted.

"But she's needin the help of Lucy McVay," he answered, glowering. "Don't you hear her cry?"

Lucy turned back into the room. "Then tell that black woman to fetch the kettles to this fire, and some whitenin cloths and a flannel warm to the touch," she answered.

From the bed came the pleading cry again, "Jim, is that you?"

Placing her satchel near the fire, Lucy said, "Go tell that black woman three kettles, and the water a-boilin in the two of them, and one fer the coolin, and a pan and a gourd fer the usin."

Without waiting for him to answer, she went toward the bed. Amelia Boyden stared up with black, pain-racked eyes,

31

her hands clutching a rosary. Lucy put her hand on the hot forehead, brushing back the damp hair. "Hit's jest old Lucy McVay," she whispered, "come to help as best she knows." Quickly she returned to the fire and from her satchel she took out the axe, its edge keen and sharp. She took it to the bed and held it high so that Amelia Boyden could see it.

"No, no!" she cried. "Jim . . . Jim . . ."

"Sh-h-h . . ." Lucy comforted, "hit'll do hits work. Hit'll cut the pain, and the need fer cryin wild in the night." And with no more words she slipped it under the bed. Then she went back to the satchel and took out a medium-sized stone, smooth and cold, and a jar of pickles. She held the stone up before the eyes of the laboring woman. "And a cold stone to step back on ef yore heart gits longin to go too fer over Stick River," she whispered, and then held up the pickles, green and dark. "Fer what you don't want now, but there'll come a time. There'll come a time." Quickly she slipped these under the covers near Amelia's feet.

The Negro woman had come in quietly with the kettles and the pans. "And the whitenin cloths," Lucy ordered, "in the boilin water." The woman nodded.

They built the fire higher. Into the boiling water Lucy dipped her knife and scissors and laid them out, then opened her box of herbs for quick use. She worked swiftly. When all was ready she went back to her satchel again. She lifted out a bridle, its leather twisted and mauled, its metal bit bright in the fire and candlelight, and carried it to the bed. "Here," she whispered, "keep a-tearin at this, fer the strain." Amelia Boyden only looked at her with feverish

32

eyes. Roughly Lucy pulled the fingers away from the rosary as best she could and forced the leather of the bridle into her hands. "Then hold on to yore beads, ef it's to yore peace of mind. But keep a-tearin at the bridle when the feelin runs high." Amelia Boyden clutched, the rosary tangling in her fingers and in the buckles of the bridle as a new spasm of pain passed through her. Lucy returned to the fire. She and the Negress worked busily with the cloths.

Midnight passed. Outside, the rain had died down, but only for a time. Soon a new gust of rain hit the window and a shaking roll of thunder went through the Valley. The two women worked on, putting cold cloths on the sweating forehead, untangling the leather from her hands when it had to be done, with Lucy muttering, "Hit's not a night to fetch a thing natural, but Lucy's doin her part." She glanced in fright toward the windows.

Finally, a little after three o'clock, when the wick of the candle in the cup before the crucifix was almost in the tallow and the fire on the hearth had grown low, Lucy went to the window. The sky, faintly visible through the thick trees, to her sharp eyes was beginning to break. "Oh," she gasped, "the night's runnin out."

She glanced apprehensively at the flickering candle. "My time's over," she whispered to the Negress. "Bad omen to the thing, and hits maw cryin alone in the night to the man of her love, and he not answerin, and Lucy McVay in the Valley with the night runnin out." The old woman only looked at her with deep somber eyes, not moving from her place near the bed.

Quickly Lucy began gathering her things—the bridle, the axe, the stone, the jar of pickles, and her box of herbs,

33

except for the few bags she was leaving for the now sleeping woman. When she had done this, she went back to the bed. She bent over Amelia Boyden and the flanneled thing in her arms; and then with a nod to the Negress she opened the door and slipped into the hallway leading to the kitchen.

The Big Squire was seated at the table. He was coatless, and he was clutching a mug in his hands, the light from the fire setting his hair aglow. At her coming he half-rose, his eyes searching her face. "Man or animal? Red hair or black?" he whispered.

But Lucy evaded his eyes, moving frantically to her coat and shawl, her glance flying to the door. "I've got to go," she answered, terror in her voice.

"But did you fetch it?" he cried.

She nodded.

"What were it?" he asked, his hands moving uncertainly.

"Like to nothin born on land or sea," she cried.

The color drained from the Big Squire's face and his eyes turned black. Lucy edged toward her coat and shawl. The movement caught him up. "But you'll not wait for me to hold it in my hands, and it mine to hold?"

Lucy clutched her coat. "The night's runnin out."

"But . . ."

"Didn't I come to the answer of the Big Squire? An didn't I do all mortal woman could do? And now I'm pleadin and beggin . . ." her voice rose to a wail; ". . . Lucy McVay in a candle-litten house."

"But didn't you hear me say they're for peace in the house?" he roared, rising from the table and going past her toward the hallway. But before he reached the door she called wildly after him, "And bad omen to the thing, with the sun techin the Valley and Lucy McVay in it."

A swift shadow of fear passed over his eyes. "I'll fetch the horse," he said abruptly.

"No," and her voice caught him short. "I rode into the Valley on the hoss that bears the Big Squire, but Lucy McVay goes out of the Valley by foot, or more omen."

"Then . . ." and he turned back to go to a shelf near the mantel. Quickly he poured a mug of whiskey and shoved it across the table to her. "Drink," he said gruffly, and then, reaching into his pocket, he pulled out a gold piece to throw it on the table. "For the work of the night, and the thanks of Jim Boyden go with you." He bowed slightly and went out the door.

Hastily Lucy downed the whiskey, picked up the gold coin, and, throwing on her coat and shawl, she stepped out into the yard.

The sky through the limbs was beginning to show gray. A sharp wind cut through the wet leaves. The heavy mass of Little Stepper House was beginning to show an outline in the night. In a few moments, from the shadows back of the house, came the Big Squire and with him the Negro man who had assisted her from the horse. The Negro was carrying a lantern.

"He'll show you the way," the Big Squire said, "and fetch the satchel. And I say again, it's not to my likin that you go with no bed to lay your head on in the house of Jim Boyden." And he bowed again, slightly.

"But the night's runnin out," she repeated, glancing fearfully at the sky.

35

"Then the thanks of Jim Boyden ride after you," he answered, turning to the door.

The Negro led the way through the trees. The ground was rocky and covered with wet leaves, but soon they came to a kind of roadway that was easier to follow. Lucy kept her eyes on the lantern ahead. She dared not look back to see what Little Stepper House might look like in the breaking night. She only looked straight ahead, her eyes on the lantern.

She could see the thick trees along the way, the firs and pines and black hemlocks close to their way, the massive trunks of oaks and maples. Still she would not look behind her. Soon the sky became streaked with white and shafts of red; far ahead of her against the sky, she saw Hanging Rock, its mass turning red in the morning light. The sight of it quickened her steps, but not until she came over the ridge, and could see the two big boulders that marked the entrance to Little Stepper Valley at the road that ran past Dave Crockett's mill, did her heart beat easily. The Negro had reached the boulders. She called after him. "From now on I ken take the way."

He stopped, and when she came up to him he said, "De mawnin's a-pinkin in."

"Yes, and good wish to you." Taking the satchel, she ran down the road.

DAVE CROCKETT

The day after Lucy McVay's journey into Little Stepper Valley the news spread through the Cove, and before night she had callers. And before the end of the week some had walked for as much as twenty miles from back in the mountains, to hear from her lips of what she had seen and what she knew. But to Lucy it was as if knowing what lay inside the Valley were hers, and hers alone, to hold.

"Tell us, tell us," they would ask, "were it a Little Squire?"

"Time fer to tell," she evaded, "and Lucy McVay t[ ]
know."

"Then what were the Old Lady like?" they pleaded[ ]
hoping to lure her into telling them more.

Lucy looked around the room as if she were afraid some
one not present were overhearing her words. Then she
whispered, awe in her voice, "A woman cryin pope-words
to the Holy Woman and tearin at the bridle, like any Chris
tian woman."

"And the Big Squire," they pleaded. "What'd he do?"

"Hopin and wantin a thing after the way of hisself, like
any mortal man," she answered.

"And were he lovin to his wife?"

"He were the Big Squire," she answered noncommittally.

"Then hit's a dream you're livin," Will Hollister broke
out, angry at her way of knowing and not telling.

"A dream? A dream?" she cried at him, anger in her own
voice. "Weren't it Lucy McVay that the Big Squire come
fer on that black hoss of hissen? Weren't it Lucy McVay
that rode into the Valley and the lightnin a-curlin in ropes
about the way and the road? And aint it Lucy McVay that's
seen what no woman or child or man in these mountains
has seen? And the wild winds cryin, and pope-candles
burnin through the night? A dream? A dream?" . . . and
passionately she tore the goldpiece from its wrappings in
her bosom. "Look what the Big Squire give me," and she
held it up for them to see. "And I'm keepin it to go to the
Big Squire's funeral when he's killed, and the Little Squire
to ride after him."

"Then it were a Little Squire," they cried, grasping at
her words.

38

"Hit were," she had to admit.

"Were it born natural?" . . . fearful of the answer.

"Like to nothin born on land or sea," she cried, holding them with her eyes. "And it givin a yelp at the first breath to let nobody tell it what to do, and the sun touchin Lucy McVay's hind foot comin out the Valley."

"Oh," they gasped.

"Hit were jest more'n I could do to git out," she added plaintively.

And that's all Lucy McVay would tell, and long after she had left Crocketts Cove to go down into the mill village of Anderstown a silent resentment lived after her. But whether Lucy would tell them or not, the Cove folk could think about what the Little Squire might be, and how he would be killed, and they began telling their children, "Ef you behave yoreself, you ken grow up to go to the Little Squire's funeral, when he's killed."

But if Lucy McVay wouldn't tell them, Old Dave Crockett could and did. He lived in a log-and-plank house directly under Hanging Rock and along the banks of Blue Snake Creek. His barn was big, and he had a great cherry tree in the back; and in front over his porch and the corner of his roof a high weeping willow swayed in the wind against the sides of his house.

Across the road was his mill. It was a two-story, gray-plank building, with an enormous overshot wheel on the outside, turned by water from Blue Snake Creek. The mill was old, older than any man in Crocketts Cove could remember. Meal dust lay on its rafters that had been lying there since long before 1800, in Dave's great-grandfather's time, and there was not too much about the Boydens, the

39

Big Squire, the Old Squire before him, and his father before him, that Dave couldn't tell if he cared to; for the Boydens had brought their grain out of the Valley for generations to Crockett's mill. "Hit'd be hard to grind a man's meal fer a hunderd years and not know somethin about them that brought the grain," Dave would say. He was thin and old and gray-haired and gentle, but no one in or near the Cove was closer to the Big Squire in his day than Dave Crockett. And after the Big Squire had been killed, there was no one closer to Little Squire Jim.

After the Big Squire's death and his strange burial, Little Jim came out of Little Stepper Valley on the Big Squire's horse to Dave's mill. The boy must have been eight years old. "His red hair come down to a little peak in the back of his neck, jest like any other little feller's," Dave said. The boy was accompanied by an old Negro man. The two of them came only twice that first year, and only twice the next. Then the Negro stopped coming altogether. When Dave asked in a moment of curiosity what had happened to the man, the boy was silent, as if he had not even heard the question. In fact, Dave insisted, in all his visits to the mill the boy had never spoken a single word. He came into the mill. He watched the transformation of grain into meal or flour. He lifted the bags onto the horse's back. He then rode back into the Valley—talking no more, Dave added, "than the sack on the hoss's back." However, after the boy had been coming for almost five years, Old Dave asked again, directly, "Where's that black man used to come with you two or three years back?"

Little Jim had just brought Blackfire to the porch edge, preparatory to throwing the sack of meal on the horse's

40

back. Dave was conscious of how muscular in the shoulders the boy was, like his father, and how like the red October leaves across the road was his hair. For a moment it seemed the boy had not heard the question. Then he turned and came back up on the porch. His words were sudden:

"Dead and put in the ground."

The voice had a husky strength about it, unusual for a boy so young.

"Where's his wife?" Dave pursued, giving vent to years of curiosity. "Seem like I recollect he had a wife."

"Dead and put in the ground."

"And wasn't there a colored boy too?"

"Went over the mountain."

"Then nobody down there in that there valley but you and yore maw?"

"About."

"Who else?"

"Eldo."

"Who's he?"

The eyes of the boy grew vague. The yellow-flecked blueness changed into a blackness. Old Dave had a feeling the boy was slipping away.

Blackfire pawed the ground impatiently.

The blueness came back into the boy's eyes. But he did not answer the question. Old Dave mumbled confusedly, "Blackfire's gitten old."

"About ready to get in the ground himself."

Dave felt he should not question the boy further, but his pent-up curiosity forced more words from him. "So jest you and yore maw and this Eldo live over there in Little Stepper Valley?"

41

"And Blackfire."

"Of course. And Blackfire. That all?"

The boy did not answer. Dave shifted his questioning. "How old are you anyhow?"

Still there was no answer.

"By now, I reckon you must be twelve or thirteen," Dave pursued.

The boy, without answering, lifted the sack of meal from the porch and put it on the horse's back, and with offended dignity went down the mill steps, walked around and lifted the rein of the horse over its head. He sprang on its back. The movement had in it the litheness of an animal.

Inside the mill a torn wheel-belt was flapping. At each revolution the loose edge of the belt made a sharp snapping in the fused rumbling of the grinding stones and ponderous wheels and cogs. Old Dave could hear its sharp flap-flap, flap-flap, flap-flap. "I ought to go shet that belt off before it breaks hitself in two," he thought.

But instead of moving to save the belt, he continued to stand in the doorway, watching the boy and horse going down the road. Soon they would reach the bend and be lost from sight. "He's jest like a wild thing, an don't invite no pryin, and I reckon I ought to be gitten used to him by now," he muttered. As he stood there, the flapping of the belt in his ears, his thoughts rumbled back to the first time he or anyone in the Cove had ever actually seen the boy, to the brightness of that June day, the redness of the cherries in the sun, and that strange, gleeful yelp trailing over the shoulders of the Big Squire as he and Little Jim galloped off down the road.

On that June day Old Dave had been standing in the door of his mill much as he was standing then, when he saw the Big Squire turn the bend and come riding toward the mill. Blackfire was young then and in the prime of his vigor, and held his head high, and the Big Squire himself could not have been over forty. It had been more than a year since Dave had seen the Big Squire, and the sight of him coming up the road warmed Dave's heart. He was hatless, his gray-and-yellow shirt open at the neck, his red hair bright in the sun, and he sat on Blackfire as if he owned heaven and hell and all the good bottomland in between. He did, too, Dave insisted, over there in Little Stepper Valley. His eye was roving, for the Big Squire had a quick eye for a pretty face or a handsome figure.

The Big Squire drew near the mill. Old Dave unconsciously dusted the meal off his chest and arms and moved hospitably forward.

"Howdy, Squire."

"Howdy, Dave Crockett," answered the Big Squire, turning into the mill yard. He was looking solemnly up at Hanging Rock, poised so high above that it seemed a part of the sky. "I reckon, Dave Crockett," he said, his eyes still straight up, "if you saw Old Hangin Rock up there a-teeterin about to fall, and about the only way to save yourself would be to vote a Republican ticket, you'd think about it mighty fast, wouldn't you?"

"Not even ef I knowed fer sure that rock was comin straight down on me, Squire," Dave answered.

The Squire laughed. Then for the first time Dave noticed, sitting up on the saddle in front of the Big Squire

43

and held securely in his arm, a child of four, perhaps five —the strangest, most solemn-faced thing Dave had ever seen. He was naked to the waist, and his shoulders were a deep tan. His face was expressionless, but the eyes were large and blue and flecked with yellow, and bright like a little fox's, and the hair was a wild, red halo.

"That the Little Squire?" Dave asked in wonder.

The Big Squire looked down at the red curls. "I reckon that's what he is."

"Reckon it'll ever grow big enough to git killed?"

"Ever hear of a Boyden man not been killed?" the Squire answered in pride.

Dave came nearer the horse. He looked at the boy closely. "The cherries are ripe in back of the house over there," he invited. "Want to go eat some?"

At the word 'cherries' a brightness flared up in the eyes, but there was no more expression or sense of comprehension in the face, Dave felt, than if he had said the same words to some wild animal sitting on a rock.

"He's not much of a talker," said the Squire.

"Is he natural?"

The Squire threw back his head and laughed. "When he wants somethin, he can talk faster than his maw can slip her beads."

Up to that minute, so far as Dave could tell, the boy had not moved a muscle. Then suddenly he squirmed in his father's arms, was on the ground, and off around the corner of the house. Dave blinked his eyes.

"That's the quickest thing I ever seed in my life. Quicker'n a fox behind a bush."

The Squire shifted his body in the saddle. "His maw

44

swears his ways come from not bein baptized. But I says to her, no pope-lovin priest is going to say words over Jim Boyden, and no pope-lovin priest is baptizin my son. It's just raw meat he needs, I tell her." The Squire's eyes grew brighter. Evidently his resentment toward his wife was more burning that day. "With that she gets on her knees and begins slippin beads and lightin candles. 'Actin like that makes the boy a bastard,' I shouts at her—" the Squire broke off. Even while he talked he had kept his eyes on the corner of Dave's house where the boy had disappeared. "Reckon I'd better go catch him before he flies," he said, moving his horse toward the house.

They found the boy up in the cherry tree behind the house, feet braced on two limbs, his hands free. With wicked speed he was pulling cherries off the branches and cramming them into his mouth, spitting out the seeds in a red cascading rattle below. The Squire rode up under the tree.

"Come down here and get on this horse," he shouted up. "You'll die of jeeters eatin cherries like that."

As if he had not heard a word Little Jim continued eating. The Squire jerked at the reins.

"Come down here, you little red-headed devil, or I'll ride up there and fetch you down."

The boy only spat a mouthful of seeds and climbed farther out, filling his mouth with both hands. The Squire in anger rubbed his hand over his head in futile scratching and bellowed, "If you don't come down here, you little red-headed bastard, I'll ride off and leave you up there till the blackbirds come by and peck out your eyes."

At that the boy stopped, and in the instant he was swing-

45

ing down, hands and feet, and standing on a low branch—in the batting of an eye, it seemed—with arms outstretched ready for the Squire to catch him. The Squire reached up and lowered him into place on the saddle before him, and put spurs into the horse. But even before the horse could spring Little Jim had raised to catch two branches of cherries in each hand and, as the horse sprang forward, he stripped the branches of cherries and leaves. Man and horse and boy were off over the ditch and down the road in clatter of steel and stones and sand and that sound of a yelp, like something wild, trailing over the Squire's shoulders.

After that never did the Squire bring the boy again. Nor did the Squire himself ride out of the Valley to the mill often. About the Cove there was talk of his riding directly over the mountains to Tateboro, and there was talk that Amelia Boyden no longer held the affections of the Big Squire. But visit or not, the Squire stayed close in the hearts of the folk about the Cove, and when four years later he was killed—he was caught with a woman near Tateboro and the woman's husband shot him—the news came as a shock. They expected him to be killed, of course, but they thought of his killing as a thing far off, not a thing in front of a man, like the falling of Hanging Rock.

However, when the details of the Big Squire's killing were known—the bullet had gone through his neck and he had died immediately—and the fact of his death could not be denied, the Cove folk gathered at Dave Crockett's mill. They made plans. They would honor him in his burial as they had in his living days. Will Hollister was delegated to go into Tateboro and accompany the body of the Squire back to the Cove. A guard of honor—Dave Crockett, Lew

46

Campbell, Thag Totten, Til Umbarger, all family heads—was to wait at the boulders that marked the entrance into the Valley and escort the body into the Valley. Every man, woman, and child would attend the burying. They would set up an open fire pit outside near the old slave houses and roast a pig and a beef. They would file through the big room of Little Stepper House and get a good look at 'all them painted pitchers of the Old Squire, and his daddy before him.' Maybe the Big Squire's wife would ask Annie Umbarger to sing a ballad about the Squire and also some Christian hymns. The ballad was to begin:

> *Oh, the Big Squire Jim were a Boyden man,*
> *And out of the Valley he come a-ridin,*
> *The Big Squire Jim were a handsome man, and a*
>   *hasty-lovin man,*
> *And on a wild hoss he went a-ridin.*

If the Squire's wife had candles 'a-burnin,' Annie was to keep her eyes closed and 'not know what she couldn't see.' But whatever might happen, at last they were going to the burying of the Big Squire.

Accordingly, at a little before noon, when it was judged that the body of the Squire was due to arrive, the guard of honor met at Dave's mill and started for the entrance to the Valley. They wore their Sunday suits. Their boots were oiled.

When they arrived at the boulders, however, they found Amelia Boyden already there. Not one of the guard had ever seen Amelia Boyden. She had never been more than a legend to them—she was Old Lady Gwynn's half-sister, and

47

the Squire never spoke of her with pleasure. They knew, though, in the way that people can know things, that she loved the Squire with a fanatical devotion. It was the one thing that kept her from being all wicked in their eyes.

She stood back of the boulders, a smallish woman, not much taller than Annie Umbarger, thin and sallow, with black, burning eyes. Whether she saw them or not the guard of honor could not tell, but when they came close to the boulders she deliberately sat down on a stump, looking down at a rosary in her fingers. Behind her stood the Negro boy and the old Negro woman.

The guard of honor went close enough for her to speak to them. But she kept her eyes on her rosary. Finally, when she did look up to glance down the road, Old Dave moved toward her. He would make her see him. She swept him with her feverish eyes, and then looked down. Dave retreated.

At last, in the late afternoon, a mule-drawn wagon came down the road. The old Negro sat in the wagon with the coffin. The undertaker was driving the mules. Will Hollister rode behind on a horse.

When the wagon reached the boulders, Amelia Boyden rose from the stump and came forward. In a harsh voice she ordered the coffin taken out of the wagon and placed on the stump inside the boulders. Then she asked the undertaker his fee. The undertaker grew confused at her abruptness, but he told her the amount. From a bag which had been resting beside the stump she counted out the sum in silver dollars, one at a time. That done, she tied the bag, unscrewed the coffin, and put the bag inside. Then, motioning to the Negroes to help her, she caught up a handle of the coffin.

The guard of honor moved forward. Dave Crockett said, "We've come to help take the Big Squire into the Valley."

Amelia Boyden stopped and, turning to look over her shoulder at him but still holding the coffin handle, said fiercely, "He's mine."

The guard of honor stopped in their tracks. "But we've come to help at the buryin of the Big Squire," Dave repeated stubbornly.

Amelia Boyden did not answer, only turned to nod at the Negroes, and the guard of honor could only stand helplessly outside the boulders watching them move slowly down the road into the Valley with the coffin of the Big Squire.

That night, however, the Cove folk met again at Dave Crockett's mill. Their resentment ran high. They were not going to be so treated. "The Squire's ourn, too," they muttered, "and he ought to be laid away with his folks a-holpin him." They took a vote. They would assert their rights. They would go to the burying of the Big Squire anyhow. "The Old Lady Boyden's never been right in the head," they argued, recalling her burning black eyes and fierce words. "She don't know what she's doin, and she don't know what's fitten."

And so, before sunup next morning, the Cove folk began streaming into Little Stepper Valley—the men with set faces, the women and children quiet but determined. Some walked, some rode mules or horses, some went in wagons. They had waited a long time for the burying of the Big Squire, and they were going to go to it.

When the first ones arrived, however, they found the doors and windows of Little Stepper House, except for the windows of one corner room upstairs, tightly closed. They hurried up to the graveyard.

A red-clay mound was already piled high in the Boyden graveyard! No marker. Not a petal of a flower. Only a red-clay mound!

In consternation they went down to the yard to meet those coming after them. They took them up to the graveyard. "Hit aint natural," they muttered. "Hit aint natural and hit aint fitten," and pointed at the newly formed red-clay mound.

In a kind of bewilderment they hovered about the graveyard, examining the other tombstones, reading the inscriptions of 'Killed' on all those marking the graves of the men —of the Big Squire's father, the Old Squire, and his father before, and his father before him. "Taint right," they muttered. "The Big Squire got killed like he was gonter, but he aint buried natural and fitten."

Then a new fear seized them. Had anybody seen the Little Squire? Lucy McVay had been at the borning of him. Dave Crockett had seen him that day when the cherries were ripe. But why hadn't he been at the boulders with his mother to bring the Big Squire into the Valley? "Maybe he's been killed, and we don't know. And there aint a Little Squire." They searched frantically about the graveyard for a short grave. "Ef she'd bury the Big Squire and let nobody know, maybe she'd not be natural enough to let the Little Squire . . ." They wouldn't say the words. They recalled Lucy Kile, who had killed her child when she went out of her head in a crazy fit.

50

They edged toward the house. But they did not go too close. Fear of the unknown gripped them. The open windows of that high corner room were the only thing that gave a sense of life to the massive brick house. They looked up confusedly. Finally Annie Umbarger said she would go closer. The folk watched her with beating hearts. She went slowly and hesitantly. She peeped in the kitchen window. Then she rejoined them. "She's in there," Annie said with husky voice, "in front of a candle, slippin beads and mumblin pope-words."

"But the Little Squire?"

"And the Little Squire's in there too, settin in front of the fire, his face whiter'n an artichoke root."

"Were his hair red fer sure like the Big Squire's?"

"Redder'n a fox's tail in the sun, but," she added with a loving caress in her words, "his face were little and sweet like."

"And were he movin?"

"No. Jest settin there." Then she looked about her into the eyes of the anxious faces. "But he sure were there in the flesh."

"Then we're aimed to wait till he comes out," they muttered.

However, when the sun came close to the brow of Hanging Rock in the far distance, and the shadows began to grow long under the trees, and still the door of Little Stepper House did not open, the folk began to talk of getting out of the Valley before dark. They did not dare think of what might befall them if they were caught in Little Stepper Valley in the blackness of the night, and 'that woman in there, out of her mind, sayin pope-words.'

51

That night Til Umbarger sat in the chimney corner long after supper, his pipe unlit, watching the flames crawl along a chestnut log. He sighed repeatedly. Annie gave no answer, only shook her head over and over again. Finally Til knocked the ashes out of his pipe and untied his shoe preparatory to going to bed. "Well," he said, "we done all we could fer the Big Squire and, one way of lookin at it, we've been to his buryin."

Annie put the herbs back into the cradle and went over to the bed and pulled down the quilt. "Well, I'm not a-sayin where you've been nor where you've not been, Til Umbarger. That's to yore own way of thinkin," and she plumped a pillow resentfully. "But I aint seed the Big Squire laid out. And I aint seed him put in his grave. And, as fer me," and she gave the pillow a still sharper plump, "I aint been to the buryin of the Big Squire."

Til took off his clothes and crawled in under the feathers. But Annie was in no hurry. She busied herself about the room. She straightened up the chairs. She brushed the coals further into the fireplace. Then she undressed slowly. Finally, when she had extinguished the lamp, she went to the window and looked out.

Til said kindly, "There's nothin you ken do about the buryin of the Big Squire now, Annie."

But Annie still looked out the window. "Til," she finally said, "why you reckon them winders of Little Stepper House was open to the air, and hit not come spring time?"

"Maybe hit's the sleepin room of the Little Squire and they never got around to closin em."

"Maybe."

"What you thinkin, Annie?"

"I jest keep thinkin about a woman what loves her man an don't know which way to turn."

"Now, Annie. Her ways're not our ways."

Annie continued to look out the window toward the dark hills. "Til," she murmured, "hit wouldn't faze me one minute to see the Big Squire come ridin out of the Valley some dark night on that black hoss of hissen."

"Now, Annie," Til said. "He's been killed and he's a-sleepin in his grave alongside of his daddy."

"Well, I aint seed him in his grave."

"Come on to bed, Annie," Til urged. "When the Little Squire gits killed we ken make sure to git to his buryin on time."

"I jest keep a-thinkin about them open winders," Annie answered. "And that woman in front of them candles."

"Well, anyhow, the Little Squire's a fact," Til answered.

Annie nodded to the dark hills. "Yes, that I've seen with my own eyes."

After the Big Squire's death a deeper mystery lay over the Valley, as impenetrable as the forest that climbed the sides of Little and Big Stepper Mountains and lined the entrance between the two boulders into the Valley; but the strange burial of the Big Squire continued to prey on the minds of the Cove folk. A few even climbed the cliff above Hanging Rock to see if 'sperits or sech were connivin in there.' But the climbers could discern nothing except the wild trees and low hills and black shadows. Til Umbarger climbed to the cliff one stormy night when the lightning was cutting like flames across the Valley. He climbed out to the very edge of the fissure near Hanging Rock. He was certain he would see wild sights and fire in the Valley by the storm-light. But the rawness of the rain and the dread of tipping loose Hanging Rock were greater than his desire to know what was going on in the Valley, and he came back down to stop at Old Dave Crockett's mill to dry himself. He sat moodily silent. Old Dave could not pry a word from him.

However, in the autumn after the Big Squire's death the old Negro came out of the Valley to Dave Crockett's mill. That was startling enough. But with him was Little Squire Jim, astride the Big Squire's black horse, sitting, even with a sack of grain in front of him, with the same air that had been so characteristic of his father, as if the world and all within were his. He wore no shirt. His shoulders and torso were brown to a berry. His hair glowed red about his solemn boyish face.

He slid off the horse and stood in the road. For his eight or nine years he was not large, but Dave was conscious of how lithe he was of muscle.

"Howdy, Little Squire."

The boy only stared back at Dave with expressionless countenance. For the moment Dave thought of the first time he had ever seen the boy, on the saddle in front of his father the day the cherries had been red in the sun.

"Want to come into the mill and see the meal come out?" Dave invited.

Little Jim only stared at Dave from the other side of the horse.

Dave helped the Negro with the grain.

The next week, however, when the boy and the old man returned for the meal, Little Jim did not wait for an invitation. He slipped swiftly off the horse and came up on the porch. When Dave was busy inside, the boy went to the door and stood shyly by the doorframe. Dave pretended not to notice him, but he had the feeling that the boy's eyes were following him as would the eyes of a lonely little animal. After a time, when it seemed a natural thing to do, Dave went close and put out his hand to cup the head, as he might to any child. Instantly the boy slipped outside and waited on the other side of the horse until the meal was brought out, eyeing Dave gravely from under the horse's head.

But the next year when he and the Negro made the trip, the boy came into the mill uninvited. He went closer to Dave of his own volition. And the next year, when he came alone, he stayed longer in the mill than Dave had ever remembered his staying. But Dave did not again make the error of intruding upon the boy's shyness. Instead, by subtle means, he encouraged him to go about the mill, do anything he wished.

The machinery fascinated him—the big overshot wheel outside the mill, turning slowly, emptying its buckets with a slush of water. Over a hundred and twenty-five years it had turned with that grinding, slushing sound, its rotting parts replaced from time to time, itself now totally new, and yet old and the same, like an aged person who looks back upon his youth and sees himself a child, different in form and mind, yet possessed of a certainty of sameness

55

and a sense of inner immutability that stays permanent though all the outer particles shift their substance and form.

With solemn eyes Little Jim watched the great wheel turn in the water. He followed the shaft inside to trace out the countershafts with their dogwood cogs, slick as oil, turning steadily. He watched the grain go into the hopper above; watched it feed into the grinding stone mill wheels that turned with slow regularity, breaking the grain into particles; watched these particles, by their own spinning, creep out through the thin opening of the edges of the two grinding stones, to be sifted and sacked into new form— changed, yet the same. Little Jim watched the process quietly. Sometimes Dave pointed out the details, explained the principles. The boy listened quietly. Never once did he respond vocally to anything Dave said, and the latter began to accept the idea that the boy couldn't talk. And yet he remembered that the Big Squire had said he could, if it suited him to do so.

For two years the marvel of the wheels and the transfer of the power of Blue Snake Creek into meal fascinated him. Then he ceased to be interested. Only the quiet devotion to Dave which had sprung up seemed to continue. After the old Negro ceased to come with him, the devotion seemed ever stronger, until that October day when Dave began questioning him, and said, "By now you must be twelve or thirteen," to which the boy had responded only with offended silence, and left him leaning in the doorway.

Dave shifted his shoulder. From inside he could hear the scarred belt flapping more insistently. "I shouldn't of pried," he muttered. "He's jest not natural, that's all—the quarest thing that ever growed up in these mountains."

The flapping of the belt inside reached a sharp peak of sound. "I ought to go shet that belt off," he repeated to himself. It stopped. "Hit's broke," Dave said aloud. . . . The boy and horse turned a bend and were lost out of sight.

Dave Crockett had good reason to repent his prying. Jim did not return to the mill for over two years. But sometimes in the night when the storms were high, and thunder and lightning shook Old Hanging Rock, Dave would hear galloping hoofs through the Cove. "Hit don't sound like the Big Squire's old hoss," he said to his wife. Then folk began telling him that they had seen Little Jim in the daytime ride through a meadow on a wild bay stallion. He rode low over the horse's neck, urging it to extraordinary speed. He never came near anyone, however. Always he was only a flash at some far end of the road or field. When Old Dave would hear this he would shake his head, muttering, "I shouldn't of pried. I shouldn't of pried."

ANNIE UMBARGER

The Big Squire had been a possession of the Cove folk. The Little Squire became more than a possession. He became something in their hearts and imaginations. Lacking things about him to touch, or to hold to, or even to recount, the folk made up for them by fancy. Since he never came close to anyone except Dave Crockett, they seized the most trifling of things about him to dwell upon. A glimpse of him bent low over the red stallion, so low his own hair was mingled in the horse's mane and one seemed the other; or the sound of his passing in the night, the hoofs of the stallion rattling the stones of the mountainside, and the next day hoof marks left clear in the soft loam of the bottomland—these were enough to set their hearts beating.

There was one jarring note, however, and that came from the Tottens.

The Tottens' land began with bottomland and climbed the sides of Sleeping Father Mountain in wooded and cleared patches, up to the very edge of Hanging Rock. The Tottens, three brothers—Thag, Lennert, and Broat—and a sister—Maybelle—welcomed no one on their land. 'No trespassin Tottens' they were called. The Cove folk knew why. The Tottens grew more corn than they had ground into meal, and the Cove folk knew still-smoke when it rose above trees; and they also knew what was inside the pumpkins which Lennie Totten took into Tateboro at intervals. A large pumpkin could hold a gallon jug of almost anything. That is, if anyone wanted to use his corn that way.

Thag Totten, eldest of the three brothers, was a church man, a Foot-washing Baptist, and a man of deep convictions. He was against Annie Umbarger for stopping blood and curing the sick by 'readin out the Bible.' "Hit's trespassin on the rights of the Lord," he maintained.

Annie Umbarger could forgive Thag's denunciation of her in the church for using the Bible for her cures, "fer anybody has a right to their own way of thinkin," but she couldn't forgive a Totten's objection to Little Jim's horse tracks across their land.

One night in March when the winds were curling around Annie Umbarger's chimney, she and Til sat before their fire. Til was smoking his pipe; Annie was working with herbs. She examined each leaf carefully, holding it close to her nose for odor, and then she rubbed the leaves between her thumb and finger to powder them before tieing them into little bags.

A flash of lightning showed through the window. A distant stroke of thunder rolled over the mountain tops. Til glanced uneasily up at the window.

"Little Jim's grandaddy was killed in a streak of lightnin and folks heared him yellin fer miles around fore they could git to him." He glanced at Annie. "Reckon we'll hear him yellin tonight, and ridin the wind?" he pursued.

Annie held a herb up to the light to inspect it better. She did not answer.

"Annie, what you frettin about? You aint spoke a word in a hour, jest set there rockin and rockin and sighin and sighin. Is it still about Sister Lucy down there in town?"

"I'm not frettin about Lucy goin down there and takin up with town ways. Not no more."

"Then what you frettin about?"

Annie didn't answer for a time. Then she burst out, "Hit's her havin dealins with a Totten man."

"But she's been buyin punkins from Lennert Totten a long time, and hit aint tore yore peace of mind."

"No. I don't lose my peace of mind when a Totten grows more corn than he takes to Dave Crockett's mill fer grindin. And I aint losin my peace of mind fer the killin of Bide Loman. Maybe Bide Loman knowed too much an didn't keep his mouth shet. I never lost my peace of mind over Thag Totten's way with Mary McClanahan, and I never lost my peace of mind when Thag Totten stood up

60

in church and talked agin me fer readin out the Bible and stoppin blood. Hit's no more than a Totten's good fer, I reckon; but when a Totten takes up words agin Little Squire Jim fer his hoss a-goin acrost his land to git to Hangin Rock—" Annie stopped. She could not find words to give expression to her gnawing resentment.

Til did not answer. He didn't want to stir her to further anger against the Tottens. Finally he said, in an attempt to calm her, "I'm not wantin the Little Squire to git killed fore his time, either."

"Ef anybody ken set on Old Hangin Rock in the lightnin, I reckon the Little Squire ken," Annie retorted.

"But his grandaddy wont a match fer the lightnin."

"Little Squire Jim is different."

"I know."

"And ef his grandaddy can ride the lightnin fer fifty years after he's died, and set the mountains to ringin with his yellin when the wind blows in the night, Little Jim ken set on Hangin Rock."

Til leaned forward and relit his pipe. A puff of smoke bulged out into the room, and then was sucked back. Then he looked up quickly. Annie's ears, however, had been sharper. She had her eyes on the window, her head cocked to one side.

"What's that you heared?" Til whispered.

Without answering Annie went to the window. Standing so no shadow from the light could fall outside, she peered through the window. Til came up behind her. "What you see?" he whispered.

"Look. Next to my lilac bush," she breathed.

Til peered out. The skies were black, and black shadows

61

hid the trees. The lightning cut across the sky. Clearly, undeniably, there beside the lilac bush was a horse and rider. There was no mistaking. "It's him. And he's come close to the house," she whispered. "Our house."

Til nodded. "Reckon we'd better go and ask him in?" Annie shook her head. "Let's wait."

In the minutes their breathing grew quiet. The shadows became blacker. When they could stand it no longer, Til went to the door. He opened it. "Howdy, Little Squire," he called. "Come in and set a while." There was no answer. He went out to the lilac bush. No one was there.

However, early next morning, at dawn, Annie searched the ground. Next to her lilac bushes were heavy hoof marks. They led across her garden. She ran into the cabin. "Til," she called, "he were here. He were in Annie's garden."

Til went outside and looked with her. He nodded his head. "Hit's shore his signs." He looked at Annie happily.

"And in a body's yard fer a visit in the night," she added. Then her eyes clouded. "You reckon he was needin and wantin Annie fer somethin?"

Til looked away. He couldn't give the answer.

It must have been in Jim's fifteenth year when Old Dave Crockett looked out his mill door in the afternoon and saw a man in priest's robes ride up to the porch. It was Father O'Brian. He had stopped, he explained, to ask the way to Amelia Boyden's. He took a letter from his pocket to reread its directions: '. . . to Crockett's

ill and ask the old man there. If you miss him, go a mile
beyond to a road turning off to the left between two boul-
ers.'

"You mean Little Stepper place. Sure." Old Dave looked
t the vestments of the priest. "Reckon you must be her
ind of preacher."

"Yes. She's very ill, and has written me. Could you ac-
ompany me?"

"I reckon so," answered Dave, eyeing the priestly robes.

"We should hurry."

Dave called to his wife to tell her where he was going.
He busied himself in preparation, talking all the while as
f he were going off into a strange land with an unknown
companion of doubtful safety.

"You talk like you don't plan to come back," Martha
aid.

Dave looked uneasily toward the frocked priest. "I'll be
back before midnight, ef I ken."

He saddled the horse and rode with Father O'Brian to
the rocks leading into the Valley. They turned in. It was
growing dusk. The early March rains had washed deep gul-
ies in what had once been a roadway, and the streams they
passed were swollen. But they pushed on.

"Were you ever in here before?" the priest asked after
a time, leaning over his horse to miss a low branch.

"Fer the Old Squire's buryin, and when the Big Squire
were killed," Dave answered. "Boydens lived in the Valley
a long time, longer'n anybody about the Cove ken think
back."

Father O'Brian did not answer. They rode on in silence.
Finally Dave added: "The big house, the Hall, built fore

63

Revolution time, was over in Virginny, through the gap a tother end of the Valley. This place we're goin to was th 'second house' in the old days. Some kind of law-fight be tween the Old Squire's daddy and a cousin. The cousin go the Hall over in Virginny and the Old Squire's daddy go Little Stepper House and the Valley and the furniture. Th upstairs rooms of Little Stepper is packed to the ceilin with plunder, I allers hear tell. And old Henry Clay used to come in here in the days of his oratin, when the Boyden took pride in their hosses and the race track were fer usin.'

They came to a deep twist in the roadway, dipping down into a stream that nearly touched the horses' bellies in crossing. Trees and bushes grew almost across the way When they came up to a higher bit of ground, Father O'Brian asked:

"Who has the Hall in Virginia now?"

"Nobody," Dave answered tersely. "Toland's raiders burnt it down in the War-between-the-States. And To land's men tried to git into this valley, too. They was comin, a whole passel of em, when the Old Squire's wife— she were a widow-woman then—met em at the fer end of the Valley with every gun she could lay hands on. She spread the guns out on rocks, with jest her and a nigger to fire em. The two of em set up howlin a racket. Six of the Yankees were left on the side of the mountain to rot. She wouldn't even bury em in the ground. Said they got their selves there and they could git theirselves back, dead or no. You ken see their bones ef you look in the day time, I hear tell. The old lady knowed guns and she knowed hosses, too, in her day. She were a Braxton woman from over Virginny."

64

The roadway began to get more open. "We're gitten there," Dave said.

Through the trees ahead, against the dusky sky, they could see now the great mass of Little Stepper House. Soon they could even make out the heavy columns that ran on three sides, holding up the high porch roof. But there was an air of desertion about the house. They drew into the yard.

Father O'Brian dismounted and stepped across the porch. He knocked on the front door with his fist. The thickness of the door made the sound heavy and dull. He waited.

"Reckon she's dead a'ready," Dave said from the steps, but at the moment of his speaking they heard a movement from inside. Someone was trying the lock. The lock was too old or too rusty, and a voice called through, "Come to the back."

When Father O'Brian and Old Dave went around to the wing in the back they found the kitchen door open. Father O'Brian entered first. The room was lighted by flames in a great stone fireplace. Little Jim stood near an inner door in the dim shadows. Dave could not distinguish his features, but he was conscious of how much the boy had grown since he had seen him three years before and of how his shoulders had filled out, and for a moment Dave had a feeling it was the Big Squire standing there.

"I'm Father O'Brian," said the priest. "I've come to see your mother."

Without answering, Little Jim threw open the inner door and went ahead into a half-lighted hallway. Father O'Brian followed. Dave remained in the kitchen. He seated himself near the fire. The large copper kettle and the flames eating about the iron crane made him think of Little Jim's hair and of the wild stallion of which he had heard so much. He looked around him uneasily, the fear rising in him that the horse might be in the room at that very moment. A candle under a crucifix in the far corner flickered, but Dave would not look at it with a straight gaze. He turned back to the fire under the kettle.

After a time Father O'Brian came back into the kitchen. At the expression on his face Dave impulsively said, "Hadn't I better git Annie Umbarger? She ken do things in her way fer the sick."

The priest shook his head. "I shall prepare to administer the last sacrament."

Dave felt a chill go over him. It was not clear in his mind what might be implied by the words of the priest, and he heard himself saying, "Then I'd better be gitten on back. Martha'll be frettin."

He found himself outside in the yard. He made ready to mount his horse.

"Beds all over the place."

The words were so sudden that he sprang into his saddle; then he checked himself. The voice was Little Jim's. He turned. In the starlit darkness he could see the outline of the boy's face. He could even have reached out and touched him, he was so close.

"Plenty of beds," came the offer again.

"No, Jim. But ef there's anything I ken do, you let me know."

"I'll be proud to be beholden to you," the boy said.

Dave held the rein tight in his hands. Perhaps the boy needed him to stay. Perhaps there was something he could

66

do to help. However, when he looked up again, the boy was gone. It was as if the shadows had reached out and caught him up in their blackness. Dave pushed his horse toward the road.

The next morning, near noon, Father O'Brian drew up in front of the mill. He explained that Amelia Boyden had died near five that morning, and he wanted to know if Dave would go, or find someone to ride into Tateboro and have an undertaker come out and prepare her for burial.

Dave nodded.

"The boy won't leave the house," the priest went on. "I think he feels that he must guard it with his own body."

"Maybe he's afraid you'd git to roamin and git lost in some of them upstairs rooms."

The priest smiled. "It's possible in that house. Even the halls on the first floor are interminable." His face grew serious. "I told the boy I would ask you to see someone about coming out to prepare her for burial."

"You tell the Little Squire," said Old Dave, "hit'll be a favor to me to do somethin fer him."

It did not take long for the news of Amelia Boyden's death to spread through the mountains, and when the Cove folk heard the news they dropped their work and made hurried plans. There was no taking a chance this time. They sent watchers into the Valley to stay the night, and at the time set by Father O'Brian for the funeral they crowded around the graveyard and the barns near Little Stepper House. However, they did not get too close to the house. They eyed from a distance the kitchen door and the open windows of the upstairs corner room. "Hit's the Little Squire's room," they murmured in awe, and remembered

67

that the windows had been open the same way on the day of the Big Squire's funeral.

Near noon Father O'Brian opened the kitchen door. Those closest craned their necks to peer into the kitchen. They thought they could see a few flickering candles. At a sign, those chosen by Old Dave to bear Amelia Boyden to her grave went toward the door. The others hurried to the graveyard. When the six brought Amelia Boyden up the hill the folk, as if in single impulse, moved to the far side of the grave, leaving one end completely open for the procession. They stood silent, and afterward went home to whisper about the strange happenings on that blustery March day at the funeral of Amelia Boyden. They talked about it quietly for days, for years, in whispers, recalling that when they were lowering Amelia Boyden into her grave and the priest was standing with a handful of red clay saying prayers out of a book in pope-language—they heard a sudden rattle of stones and steel in the high March wind, and through the broken hedges of the Boyden yard the carriage of Julia Gwynn appeared, careening and sawing, the horses' hoofs making dull thuds in the spongy ground. The folk moved closer together, startled, as if an apparition from hell had appeared—the coachman in silk hat on the box, black horses in glistening harness pawing the ground, and the apparition itself in black furs sitting in the back seat, hair glaring bright under black plumes. For a moment the horses seemed almost to ride upon the open grave. Then the coachman pulled them to a stop.

Julia Gwynn climbed out of the carriage. She made no move to come close, however, but stood back—a black-dressed figure with rosary in her fingers, the horses biting

heir bits at her back and breathing hard. She began slipping the beads, mouthing her own thoughts with thin
painted lips, unheedful of the priest and his words.

The first red clods hit the pine box in the grave.

Julia Gwynn turned, climbed into her carriage, and, in
rattle of wheels, her corseted back stiff in the center of the
carriage seat, she disappeared through the broken hedge as
precipitately as she had come.

But it was the way Little Squire Jim disappeared before
their very eyes that stayed embedded in the minds of the
folk, to be recalled by them when they hovered around a
smoking lamp or lay late at night in bed with their wives,
listening to the rain and wind and roll of thunder amid
jagged edges of lightning through the rain and trees, and
the clatter of a horse in furious gallop passing in the night.
"There goes Little Squire Jim wild-ridin, tryin to git hisself killed by lightnin like his grandpa . . ." And sometimes the answering whisper, "Hit'd be a sight easier to git
shot over a woman like his daddy than tryin to run into a
streak of lightnin . . ." And then they would draw closer
and think about the day at Amelia Boyden's funeral, with
Old Lady Gwynn rattling her beads and mouthing prayers
and Little Squire Jim standing at the head of his mother's
grave, his feet wide in colossal stance, that strange suggestion of completely formed grace about his body, his face
expressionless, his hair wild in the wind.

Age seemed strangely inconsequential in his face, for
those about the grave, hearing in confusion the rattle of
Julia Gwynn's rosary and the strange words of the priest in
the winds, were caught and held by Little Jim's eyes, wide
apart, enormous and encompassing; and yet in the moment

69

of their staring they saw them shade from blue into a shadowy blackness; and his face seemed to grow large and unnatural; and in the minds of the watchers there was the sudden fall of the red dirt from the priest's hand upon the pine cover of the coffin in the hole, and the eyes and face of Little Jim fading, disappearing, just being not there; and when they shook their heads, he was gone, and those on the fringe of the crowd saw him crossing the field into the woods, not running or fleeing, just disappearing in the way the redness of a fox loses itself in the brown leaves and trees, leaving nothing except suddenly accurate things close by, like Old Lady Gwynn turning sharply to climb into her carriage and disappear through the broken hedge about the burying ground.

The folk near the grave moved uneasily and whispered to one another, not sure even of their words, "Old Lady Gwynn got here after all," and there were answering nods. "Musta drove across the country since sunup." And then a little more surely, "Hit's time she got here, at the buryin of her own sister." "Half-sister." "Half-sister, then." They looked doubtfully at the grave of Big Squire Jim, expecting to hear him shift deep under the ground and maybe rear up and say, "Get that connivin bitch away from my grave and out of my house." They shifted uneasily. "You reckon . . ." and they would have spoken of Little Squire Jim's disappearing, but abruptly they talked of Old Lady Gwynn again, and only when they got home in quiet safety behind closed doors did they talk of the boy, fearful of mentioning something that hadn't existed, perhaps.

"Did you see Little Squire Jim there?" asked Annie Umbarger of her husband, furtively stirring the fire. "Did

70

you?" he asked in reply. She nodded. "As sure as I'm standin here holdin this skillet in my hand." Til Umbarger looked uneasily about the closely locked room, as if he feared to hear his own words. "I could a-swore he was big as a mountain shadow, and then I couldn't even be sure he were even there." He looked at his wife as if not completely certain even of her. "Let me tech that skillet, Annie." She lifted it toward him, but she held onto it, too, and with it caught between them Til whispered: "Yes. I saw him, too, standin there, feet wide apart, about like any growed man, except he was a boy. I know. Everything the same, like this skillet. Except that red hoss of hissen wont there, pawin the ground."

"Old Lady Gwynn's was enough hosses fer one funeral," said Annie, "and I'm glad the Big Squire's wife is dead and a-layin up among the Boyden women that's died in their own way, and the Boyden men what's been killed in their own ways, too. Little Squire Jim'll be next, I reckon." She looked toward the closed door.

"Hit's locked," Til whispered.

"Hit wouldn't faze me ef the Big Squire came walkin in, lock or no lock."

Til's face paled. "He's layin in his grave."

"Well, I fer one aint never seen him put in his grave," Annie answered.

They went about their supper quietly, and afterward Til took out his pipe and sat close to Annie's chair. To keep herself occupied, Annie got her box of herbs and began working with them. Outside the winds whistled. Heavy slashes of rain beat against the logs outside. The flames

71

grew brighter and cast a glow over the hearth and the peppers and onions and herbs hanging from the rafters near the mantel.

"Why you reckon not a Totten man were at the buryin?" Annie asked.

Til looked up. "Maybe Thag aint liked the way the Old Lady Boyden acted at the Big Squire's dyin . . ."

"That'd never stop a Totten," Annie answered.

A new swish of rain hit the glass. A distant roll of thunder, far over the mountain, echoed. "Hit were on a night like this the Old Squire tried to ketch a bolt of lightnin in his hand, and hit were too much fer even a Boyden man—" He stopped. Annie's head was turned to one side, listening. "What you hearin?"

Annie's eyes were on the door. She held her hands still. "I heared a hoss."

Til got up and went toward the door. "You reckon hit's—" he began, but at that moment from the yard came a short "Howdy, Til Umbarger."

"Hit's Thag Totten," Til breathed.

"A Totten man's not welcome to come in my house," Annie answered. "But open the door and ask him what he wants, ridin up in a body's yard and makin their heart turn over in their ribs."

Til lifted the latch. Thag Totten stood outside, a horse at his shoulder. The rain had soaked his heavy coat and hat and was dripping off his thin nose and sandy mustache. His reddish-brown eyes peered past Til into the room.

"I come to ask Annie to holp me," he said.

"Then step in out the rain an do yore askin," commanded Til. "We aint seed you at the buryin of Old Lady Boyden."

Thag came inside, but only far enough for Til to close the door. His eyes sought out Annie.

"I'm wantin Annie to come read out the Bible," he said abruptly.

Annie stared at him in surprise. "Aint it you, Thag Totten, that stood up in church on baptizin day sayin words against me? Sayin I'm a-doin sin stoppin blood by readin out the Bible? Trespassin on the rights of the Lord?"

"I aint sayin them words again to my dyin day, Annie," Thag answered. "Little Maybelle's sick, and we aint knowin which way to turn."

"Been wearin her out with work fore she's grown, like yore daddy did yore maw," Annie snapped.

"Little Maybelle aint made to do more'n she wants," Thag tried to defend.

"I know. I know," Annie murmured. "Like her maw took to plowin hill corn—up to the very minute little Maybelle was born. Born right in the cornfield."

"My daddy had his own way of doin," Thag said. He took a step nearer, his voice pleading. "Little Maybelle's talkin out of her head, and runnin hot and cold. And I'm askin you, Annie Umbarger, to come and read out the Bible. And I'll be mighty beholden to ye fer comin."

"How long's she been runnin hot and cold?"

"Goin on two days."

Annie stood up. "Til, git me my coat, and my shawl." She moved to the cradle in the far corner. "I'm not a-doin this fer you, Thag Totten. And I'm not a-doin hit fer no

73

man that's kin to Thag Totten's daddy. . . ." She got on her knees before the cradle and began hunting in its corners.

"I'll be mightily beholden to you," Thag repeated, his eyes on Annie.

From the cradle she brought out a Bible, wrapped in heavy wool, and a box. "I'm a-doin hit fer yore maw." She lifted the lid off the box and moved the bags inside it with her finger. "Little Maybelle cough fore she run fever?"

Thag nodded.

Annie went to the mantel and searched out a few bags of her fresher herbs, placed them in the box, and putting the Bible and box under her heavy coat she stood at the door.

"I brung the hoss to fetch you," Thag said.

Annie bristled. "Thag Totten, I been walkin these mountains day and night fer fifty years without ridin a Totten hoss, and I'm like to keep doin it." She stepped out into the rain.

Thag followed behind, leading the horse. The rain beat about them. The soaked leaves and the grass and the branches caught at their coats and boots. They went up rocky paths, over swollen streams. They picked their way over stones and logs. Annie never faltered in her direction; not until she reached a ridge did she stop and wait for Thag to catch up.

"This here's yore land line. You git in front and lead the way."

A flash of lightning lit up the valley—the bottomlands, the open fields near the Totten house, the slope above the house, the shoulder of Sleeping Father Mountain, and on

74

to the far north, Hanging Rock, jutting hard into the sky.

Annie followed Thag down into the Valley. When they came close to his house, he called out. The door opened and a sixteen-year-old boy peered out. "Take the hoss to the barn, Broat," Thag said.

Inside, a fire was blazing. An oil lamp burned low, its chimney smoked dark. The room was in disorder. On a bed in the corner, under a pile of quilts, a girl lay mumbling in fever. The third brother, Lennert, a man in his middle twenties, unshaven and thin, stood near the bed in the shadows. His small eyes were furtive, and his face was disagreeable.

Thag spoke sharply to him. "Annie's come to read out the Bible fer little Maybelle, Len. And I'm beholden to her."

Annie threw off her shawl and coat and went to the bed. "Hold the lamp close," she said. She pulled the quilt back from Maybelle's face. It was a pretty face, small-featured, with auburn hair that curled about the flushed cheeks and forehead. "I caint git it done—I caint git it done, I tell you," she mumbled, beginning to whimper.

"Bring a table next to the bed," Annie ordered. "Not much time."

Thag brought the table.

"And Len, you go git some spring water's not been teched with breath of man nor beast and set it boilin on that fire."

She hastily unwrapped her herbs and Bible and laid them on the table. To Broat, who came in from the barn, she said, "Fetch me a lamp aint smoked black." When she had all her things in order, and Len had brought in the

75

water and placed it over the coals, she ordered: "Put a lid over it. Now, all of you. Stand away from my things. And you, Thag, git over there in the corner by the fire, jest as far away from things as you ken git."

The three brothers, close together near the fire, watched her open her box and place it near the Bible. She closed her eyes. She laid one hand on the breast of Maybelle. With the other she held the Bible in such a way that when she released it, it would fall open. Her lips moved. Then she let the Bible fall open. Blindly her fingers ran over the page until there was a compulsion for them to stop. She turned to search the words under her fingers. The brothers by the fire watched with fearful eyes. In the half-light their faces were all cut from the same mold—narrow and thin, with eyes small and red-brown following Annie's every move as she searched the words on the page. Without raising her eyes she reached into her box of herbs. One small bag after another she placed on the open Bible. Then she bent over Maybelle, so close that her face almost touched the hot cheeks. She glanced at the bags on the page. She straightened up and turned on the brothers. Her eyes burned bright.

"Somebody in this room aint believin. Anybody aint believin, git out the room. Git out the house. Git far away as you ken git."

The faces of the three brothers grew pale in the dim light. Outside, the rain beat on the windows. A crack of thunder shook the house. She waited. Not one of them moved.

Hastily she put all the herbs back in the box and closed the Bible. Then with closed eyes and moving lips she again

76

let the book fall open. Eyes closer to the page, she hunted out new words, chose new bags from the box and set them in a row at the top of the page. Then she turned to the child, searched her face, listened to her breathing. She turned back to the Bible. "Hit's a-workin right now," she whispered. "Hit air comin out right. Git me a whitenin cloth, and a cup fer mixin. And fetch me the water's not been touched by breath of man nor beast."

When the hot water was brought, she mixed the curled leaves and powdered roots and put them between layers of cloth. She placed the poultice on Maybelle's chest and throat. A pungent odor began to fill the room. Maybelle writhed under the quilt.

Annie mixed a dull powder in water. She brought it close to her nose to test its odor. In the movement she stopped. She turned her head to listen. There was a galloping of hoofs down in the meadow. The sounds came closer; then veered, going farther away, going up the mountain back of the barns. Maybelle cried out suddenly in terror.

Lennert moved. "Damn that hoss," he muttered angrily, "stompin my fields and ridin by when little Maybelle's—"

He did not finish, for his eyes fell on Annie, who had turned from the bed and was pointing a shaking finger at him.

"Hit's a warnin, Len Totten," she cried. "A warnin. Little Jim ridin to Old Hangin Rock to git hisself killed. And little Maybelle cryin out in the warnin."

Len stared at her stupidly. But her shaking finger was still upon him, her voice rising. "Git down on yore knees, the passel of you, fore hit's too late. Git down on yore knees with yore faces to the wall. Hit's a warnin, and May-

77

belle cryin out . . . Little Jim's ridin by is a warnin," Annie said more fiercely, "a warnin fer yore mean ways of livin."

The brothers fell on their knees.

Annie turned back to her herbs. She stirred the dull mixture. It turned a brownish-green color. "Hit's a warnin," she cried, stirring the mixture to the rhythm. The moans of the child rose to cries. Annie forced a spoonful of the dark mixture into her mouth. Then she drew the quilts closer, and, pulling a rocker near the bed, she took the Bible in her lap. With one hand she held Maybelle's hands under the quilt, and with the other she began turning pages of the Bible, reading aloud from whatever place her eyes chanced to fall. As she read she mingled the phrases from the Bible with soothing words to the child on the bed. The fever in Maybelle's face burned. Her tongue grew thick. *Upon the land of my people shall come up thorns and briers; yea, upon all the houses of joy in the joyous city. . . . Then judgment shall dwell in the wilderness. . . . Blessed are ye that sow beside* . . . Annie read on and on.

When she saw Thag shift to ease the strain on his knees, Annie caught him up with a fierce goad. "Keep thinkin about yore mean ways of livin, Thag Totten. Think about all the harm you done in yore time. *Moreover the Lord said unto me, Take thee a great roll and write in it.* And think about the time when you weren't more'n a boy and you killed Lon Ashby's cow fer gitten in yore daddy's corn. Hit wont much a cow could eat, not enough to kill a man's cow fer, before givin him a chance to pay fer the corn. *Now therefore, behold, the Lord bringeth up upon them*

78

the waters of the river, strong and many. And start thinkin about Mary McClanahan."

Thag's body stiffened as if she had given him a physical blow.

"For a thousand years in thy sight are but as yesterday when it is past, and as a watch in the night. Sister Lucy and me was at Mary McClanahan's dyin, and at the layin out and buryin of the two of em, and her with no name to give her baby—"

"I aint never married nobody else," Thag answered huskily.

"Marryin nobody else aint makin Mary McClanahan come alive nor her baby neither," Annie cried. *"Thou carriest them away as with a flood; they are as a sleep.* And hit were a night like this when the two of em were dyin. And she with no daddy nor brother to take her part; jest Lucy and me a-readin out the Bible and gitten no answer fer the ways of a Totten man. And then you standin up in church talkin against Annie Umbarger. *Lord, thou hast been our dwelling place in all generations.* And when you git past thinkin about Mary McClanahan, start thinkin about Bide Loman's gitten killed and him layin in a ditch two days and no buryin—"

"Thag aint the one done that," Len cried out.

"But hit were a Totten man."

"Bide knowed too much," Len cried back.

"Bide knowed no more than other folks in these here mountains," Annie answered. "Folks know why you grow more corn than you eat and sell. *Before the mountains were brought forth, or ever thou hadst formed the earth*

79

and the world. And Bide Loman a-layin in a ditch with a shotgun hole in his back."

She rocked on, catching fragments from her Bible, exhorting now Len, now Thag, haranguing them, recalling their smallest faults, errors, sins. She leaned toward them in the light, a dwarfish fury driving their past lives before them. And when she could recall no more, she cried upon them to pray for forgiveness. She made them beat upon the floor with their hands. She exhorted them to frenzied repentance. The room was a bedlam of wails and cries and words and moans. On and on she drove them, until the three of them lay hoarse and exhausted on the floor. With their exhaustion a strange, unreal silence was in the room.

Under her quilts Maybelle had grown quiet. Annie too was still. She was listening. Down the mountainside a horse's hoofs were tearing the rocks and sod loose.

"Hit's Little Squire Jim ridin back from Old Hangin Rock," Annie whispered. "He's a-ridin back by."

The galloping hoofs came close, following the rock-strewn path nearer the house. The hoofs passed. They lost themselves far down in the meadows.

Annie started up from her chair. She pulled down the quilt from the quiet figure on the bed. She put her hand on Maybelle's face and bent over her chest. The breathing was easy.

"The fever's broke," Annie cried to the men on the floor. "Hit's broke, and hit were Little Jim's ridin by on the wild hoss of hissen that done it. Little Jim's ridin by on that wild hoss of hissen."

The brothers turned haggard faces toward her. They

80

dared not move their bodies. Their hands on the floor twitched. Annie bent again over the child, whispering, "Hit were Little Jim—Little Jim, ridin by to Hangin Rock—Little Jim . . ."

She tucked the covers secure and again turned to the men. "Git up off yore knees, and git some sleep. Little Maybelle's breathin gentle as a lamb and sleepin."

Uncertainly they rose to their feet, their eyes on Annie as if there were no meaning in her words.

"Go on to bed, and I'll set by Maybelle, watchin ef there's no change back."

Len and Broat moved to a room adjoining. They moved like figures in a trance.

"You too, Thag Totten."

"I'm a-settin up with little Maybelle alongside you, Annie Umbarger," he said.

"Set by the fire, then," she said. She turned back to the child. "She's sleepin. I hate to tech her to loose the things on her chest. I'll leave them be," she murmured. She seated herself by the bed and opened the Bible.

When streaks of rose and yellow showed in the sky outside the window and the room grew pale, Annie said, "Thag, go wake up them two brothers of yourn and tell em to stir around." And when Len and Broat came in the room she instructed: "You, Broat, when you git yore stock fed, git on a hoss and ride over to my house and tell Til I'm stayin as long as little Maybelle needs me, maybe a week, maybe longer. They's things fer a woman to do."

Broat swayed and rubbed his chin. His hands shook. "The stock ken wait." He was gone before she could add anything more.

81

"And you, Len," Annie went on, "git water to the house and on the fire, and git rags to wash this floor." She glanced around the disordered room. "You're gonna wash and clean up this house. An don't figure on gitten away fer nothin else fer a day or two till hit's done."

Lennert's surly face for a moment did not give answer.

"You heared my words," Annie said sharply.

"Hit's jest this way since Maybelle's been sick."

"Jest like I said," Annie interrupted, without looking at Thag. "A passel of triflin men sittin around lettin a girl not more'n a child wait on you. Why don't you git out and git you a woman to do yore housework, ef you don't want to do hit yoreself?"

"I aint found a woman'll marry me," Lennert answered.

"Hit's yore mean ways. A Totten's a Totten since I ken remember, but you're gonna change yore ways as long as I'm around this house."

"He'll do more'n you ask," Thag interrupted. "Hit's jest his way to argue. He aint got sweetnin ways, but he aint one not to stick to his kin."

"I'll see what I see," Annie answered. "And you, Thag, do around to suit yoreself. Little Maybelle's got pneumony deeper'n I feel easy to say, and it'll take you and me and the whole passel of you men folks to bring her back safe. The Lord's done his part. And Little Jim's done his part." With that she blew out the lamp and turned back to Maybelle, crooning: "Yes, little lamb. Don't you fret. Old Annie's gonna git you up and singin again. Jest swallow some of this. Hit'll make you sleep and when you're well you ken come see Annie's flowers. The blue-eyed grass and the trillies'll bloom, jest fer you, and the dawg-toothed violets and valley-lilies'll stir to the look. And maybe Little Jim'll come ridin by to fetch you home on his wild red hoss. Little Jim'll fetch you a-ridin on his wild red hoss."

A few days after the funeral of Amelia Boyden, Dave Crockett was dusting out the sacks in the loft of his mill. The air was thick with the mist of flour and meal, and from the high rafters the cobweb beards waved lazily with their incrustations of grain. "I've come to give you somethin," Dave heard at his back. He turned abruptly, and through the flurry of meal he saw Little Jim standing at the head of the ladder into the loft. He was holding toward Dave an old handwoven basket.

Old Dave was so surprised that he automatically took the proffered basket. In it were six heavy silver goblets. The boy had made some attempt to rub them bright, but the old silver was still dark. Their heaviness weighed Dave's hand.

"You oughtn't to give me these, Jim. They're silver things."

"I'm beholden to you for comin to help me."

"I was glad to do hit, Jim. Hit were a favor to me. But ef that's the way you feel, I'll take em and be proud you give em to me." He then added hesitantly: "You must be mighty lone up there in that there valley. All by yoreself. Whyn't you come down and visit with folks and pass the time of day? Glad to have you. Set and eat a bite with folks."

83

For a moment Dave thought Little Jim was going to answer; then uncertainty showed in the boy's eyes, and he turned abruptly and went down the ladder before Old Dave could say more; and when Old Dave reached the porch, only hoof marks in the road proved the certainty of the Little Squire's having been there. And the silver goblets in his hand.

After the curing of Maybelle there was no more talk by the Totten men against Little Jim's tramping down the corn in their bottomland. They took it as a benevolent omen. Once in a wild storm, with the lightning running in streaks up the mountainsides and the thunder loud enough to shake Hanging Rock loose, the Tottens thought they heard Little Jim's horse riding toward the Rock. Broat rushed out into the yard to see if the boy and horse reached the cliff. The lightning lit up the sky. The Rock was set aflame for a moment. He was almost sure he could see the outline of the horse upon it.

When Broat told this to the Cove folk, they shook their heads. "Hit aint right fer him to git killed before his time." And in the days that followed they kept watchful eyes for hoof marks in the fields and near their houses, and if there were no more than a scar, they took doubt for surety and treasured the fancy in their hearts.

However, in the weeks that followed, the folk around the hills and valleys began to see more of Little Squire Jim. In broad daylight he would ride suddenly up alongside some one of them, as they sat on their porches or in their doorways. For the Cove folk it was the nearest any of them had ever come to the restless bay stallion, with its foreleg

84

white to the knee, its eyes following every move of the boy when he was off its back.

Sometimes the boy would bring a gift. For what reason no one could ever know more than to hazard a guess. Perhaps something about the person to whom he brought the gift had caught his devotion. One day Annie Umbarger was in her garden when he rode up to her fence. He slipped off the horse and advanced to her, holding out a shawl intricately embroidered with gold threads running through pale-blue flowers. "Grandma Braxton's, I reckon," he said somberly. Before Annie could recover from her surprise, or even say a word of thanks, he and his horse were over the split-rail fence and going up the mountainside. The shawl lay in a silken mound on the grass.

She picked it up and when Til came home for supper she showed it to him wonderingly. "And the Little Squire were in my yard, right on top of my May lilies."

She threw the shawl over her cotton dress.

"Hit'll tech up yore eyes," Til observed in admiration, "when the evenin's pinkin in. Jest yore color."

Annie was examining the gray streak in her hair before the bit of mirror on the wall. "Wont his maw streakedy in the hair, too?" she asked.

Til did not answer.

"And wont she about my size?"

"Nothin but yore size is like the Old Lady Boyden," Til answered loyally. "Nothin but yore size."

Another time Arabel Leach was on her porch when Little Jim rode up. She was partly in the sun, and the sun caught the red in her hair. He pitched a small chest into her lap. It was a delicately carved thing with filigreed

85

bronze lock and hinges. "Jest like little foxes' teeth," she said, lifting the lid and touching the metal hinges with delight. Maybelle Totten was on the porch at the time. She was just thirteen and her eyes were glowing. She stared adoringly at Little Jim. "I'd fetch you somethin if I knowed where you live," he said. Maybelle blushed and giggled uncontrollably. Little Jim shifted uneasily.

But the Campbells, who lived near the entrance to Little Stepper Valley, told the strangest tale. They had always felt, in their way, close to the Boydens, for they had peach trees in their orchard and a mountain stream with a pump to carry the water up to the kitchen and the barn. Next to the Tottens, they had more bottomland than anyone else, and in front of their log cabin they had built a frame house with a wide hall and porch. The clapboards still showed scales of white to give proof that they had once had a coat of paint, thirty or forty years in the past.

One night in April the Campbell family was at supper, their thoughts on food and the corn to be planted soon, when suddenly they heard sounds of hoofs coming down the hill to the left of the house. Lew Campbell and his wife and his children—seven of them—paused in their eating to listen. The hoof sounds came nearer. The Campbells held their breath. The hoof sounds were in the front yard. Then on the front steps. They made a noisy clatter on the boards. On the front porch. Hoof sounds rumbled in the hall outside the dining room. It was all so sudden and clamorous that the Campbells had no time to think or move, and their consternation turned to panic when they saw through the dining-room door the head and shoulders of Little Jim's red stallion, and the boy himself sliding off the horse at his back. He was shoeless and naked to the waist, and his red hair was in a wild tangle. He held the rein of the horse in one hand, and a large silver candelabra in the other.

"I'm worn out eatin by myself."

Lew Campbell knocked his chair over in rising, but before he could speak, Little Jim moved swiftly into the room and dumped the candelabra on the table in front of Nellie Campbell.

"I give it to you," he said, moving back to the horse in the door.

Lew Campbell, righting himself, finally found voice to say, "Draw up a cheer, Little Squire, and eat a bite."

"Don't care if I do."

He dropped the rein on the floor and slipped in among the Campbell children, who could not have been more panic-stricken if a red-headed devil had come to sit in their midst. Automatically Nellie Campbell helped Little Jim to a plate. The children dared not look up even to make sure that the stallion was actually in the doorway, and their panic was heightened when with a front hoof the horse scraped the floorboards impatiently. Nellie Campbell looked desperately at her husband, and then at Jim.

"Hadn't you better tie yore hoss outside, Little Squire?" Her voice was so weak she could not be sure the boy would hear her. "Hit don't look natural in a body's dinin room."

The Campbell children kept their eyes on their plates. Thoughts of Amelia Boyden's funeral and the wild clatter of Julia Gwynn's horses, the high winds and the fall of red clods on the coffin ran through their minds. The stallion scraped the floor of the dining room again. Jim pushed his plate away and stood up. "I'm much obliged," he said. He went to the door. "Reckon I'll be eatin with you folks again." Without further words he backed the horse into the hall. The Campbells, unable to move, could only stare at the doorway, hearing the hoofs in the hall, on the porch, in the yard. When it was certain that the hoofs had lost themselves up the hillside, they rushed to the porch, looking at each other as if what they had just been through was a dream. But there were hoof marks in the yard, and scars on the porch, and in the hall; and on the table in the dining room there was a heavy, five-branched candelabra, ornately carved and dazzling.

"Hit looks a heavy thing," Lew said.

The children crowded close, not daring to touch it. Nellie finally put her finger on the base, touching the heavy carvings. "Hit's sure a purty thing to feel and look at."

She moved the lamp nearer it. The dull luster of the silver caught the rays. Nellie nodded. "And hit aint everybody ken say the Little Squire set down to the table to eat a bite with em." She searched the eyes of the children and her husband. "Hit were the Little Squire, wont hit?"

Her husband nodded. "I even seed the hoss."

"And hit were eatin at the table, too," one of the children said. No one contradicted him.

But Little Jim did not always bring a gift. Sometimes he would only ride near someone and sit under a tree close by. He gave no greeting, nor offered to answer theirs. Apparently all he wanted was just to be near someone. The

88

folk soon learned that it was best to pretend to ignore his presence, to continue their conversations or work as if he were not there. If he understood their words as they talked, there was no outward sign from him. His eyes remained fixed far off, and his face expressionless.

"And he won't take no talkin to nor askin questions, neither," Annie Umbarger ventured. "But I'm thinkin them ears of hissen under that red hair hears more'n a body'd think. I jest let him set where he sets, and I go on tendin my flowers and things."

And Annie did just that. About the mountains the folks said she had green fingers. "Ef Annie sets it out, it'll sure turn into a purty bloom," they said. She trained the vines about the porch of her log house, and along the banks of the creek that curved around her yard; and in the corners of the split-rail fence, black and velvet with age, she tufted wild flowers and ferns. Sometimes Little Jim would ride up and sit nearby under a dogwood tree. When he did so, Annie was careful not to look directly at him or to speak to him; but as if to herself she would sing aloud. "Fetchin wild phlox from Peak Creek Run, and valley-lilies, wild and sweet, out of a hill-bank sides. They'll be sweet and longin in spring night time, with the blue-eyed grass and trillies in bloom. But don't never fetch the stagger weeds, purple and blue and red to a white—pizen fer cows and mean to the birds. But they's columbine, yellow on the lip of the red, and trillies an dawg-tooth violets, and in summer they's wild butterfly and thistle blue along the meadow field. Ketch a girl with a flower. Ketch a girl with a flower when you likes, ef she's purty and sweet to tech." Annie rambled on, busy with her fingers, sing-songing

89

aloud as if to herself. "He ken hear ef he likes," she thought.

When she looked up he was gone.

Vaguely she looked about the garden, saying to herself, "Behind a bush or in a corner. Caint never tell. Ketch a girl with a purty flower. Caint never tell how he's gonna git killed. Ketch a girl with a thistle blue," and she returned to her flower-planting. "Caint never tell how he's gonna git killed."

The next day he was back, sitting on the fence. The horse was nowhere to be seen. Annie gave no indication that she saw him or that she missed the horse, but she gradually edged nearer him. Out of the corner of her eye she could see that he was watching her. "Want to see somethin nobody in all these here mountains ever seed? Nobody high nor low. And never heared of, cept me?" she asked, her sharp little face half-averted. He had his hands on the fence rail, ready to leave. "Nobody ever seed?" she asked again. Without watching to see if he heard her, she went over to a corner and knelt beside a tall hawthorn, its bush close into the fence corner; and, putting her hands behind it, she pulled back a cluster of shading mandrake leaves. "Somethin nobody seed, cept me, in all these mountains. Cept me."

Little Jim slipped off the rail. He went close and looked over her shoulder. Behind the mandrake leaves were two thin plants with yellow buds in their three-leaved stems. "Yeller trillies," she whispered, looking obliquely up at him. "Jest two of em. And nobody, I ever heared tell, has seed a yeller trillie, cept you and me."

90

Over her shoulder he eyed the flowers. There was a glint of a smile in his face.

"And sometimes when you likes, ketch a pretty girl with a yeller trillie."

He slipped back and sat on the rail.

"Ketch a pretty girl," Annie sang on, letting the mandrake leaves spring back to hide the leaves. "And nobody ever seed a yeller trillie, cept you and me."

For several days after that Annie did not see him. Then one afternoon, as she worked with her flowers, she looked up to find him sitting under a lilac bush, his red hair in the shade of the leaves, his body sprawled in her valley-lily bed, one leg drawn up to rest an arm on a knee, the other leg straight out, crushing under its weight her dog-toothed violets and russet trillium. There was a hint of a smile in his eyes and about his face as he watched her work. His closeness gave her a start, and she cried out, half in fright and half in exasperation, "Look at you, Jim Boyden, settin there like some big October mountain thing, right on my lily-bells an dawg-tooth violets, and them red trillies I fetched special out of the hill places." A wailing note came into her voice. "And breakin em all to pieces."

He rose quickly, so quickly that in her mind his getting up and the sound of mounting and the clatter of hoofs blurred themselves, and only the wrecked leaves and flowers where his body had lain were facts to Annie of his actually having been there. "He shouldn't've tore up a body's garden," she cried. She fled into the house.

The next morning before dawn she found in her yard, piled high to the size of a bush, trillium plants and dog-

91

tooth violets, masses of them, mandrakes, lady slippers, crested iris, and wild columbine. She called excitedly to her husband. "He musta tore up a whole mountain to git em. And look. Here's a flower I aint never seed before."

Til looked at the pile of flower plants and nodded. "Reckon he musta laid on yore flowers like you said, and gone like you said, too."

"I told you I know what I see," Annie said, "and I don't know what I aint seein. That's how come I'm thinkin the Big Squire aint in that grave up there. The old lady is, cause I saw the clods on her box. But I've seen no clods on the Squire's box. Wouldn't faze me to see Big Squire settin up on Old Hangin Rock some night. And I seed Little Jim layin in my flowers and gone quicker'n a mountain shadow." A plaintive note came back into her words. "But I shouldn't've spoke so quick. I shouldn't've."

"He'll be comin back, a-lettin his hoss eat up yore blooms," Til tried to comfort her.

"He ken, ef he likes," said Annie.

But Annie did not see Jim for a long time, although she heard about him. One day the Totten brothers were making hay in the lower field. Little Jim rode suddenly up. He dropped his stallion's rein under the tree and without a word took the pitchfork from Thag and began to help load the hay. He pitched so rapidly that Len Totten had to crawl on top to help Broat receive. The hay piled high. The Tottens packed it until they could pack no more. They yelled to Jim to stop. The wagon was started off toward the barn.

When the wagon returned, Maybelle was seated demurely on the front with her brothers. Her light-chestnut hair glistened red in the sun. When the wagon stopped she jumped out; taking the pail of water held down by her brother, she ran to stand under the tree. If Little Jim noticed her, he gave no sign. He began to pitch the hay in the wagon even before Broat could get the horses quiet.

His muscles rippled, his shoulders and arms gleamed in the sun. The hay piled higher in the wagon. Maybelle, under the tree, watched him as if hypnotized. When Broat breathlessly yelled to Jim to halt for a moment to give him time to catch up, Maybelle went toward Jim, gourd dipper outstretched. She stood deliberately in front of him. Little Jim paused to take the proffered gourd. He drank slowly, his eyes on her face, her breasts, her feet. Maybelle trembled slightly, and then reached up and touched his arm with her fingers. Instantly his muscles tensed. The dipper dropped. And before Maybelle and her brothers knew what he was about, he was on his horse. The stallion reared in a curve toward the mountain, but Little Jim checked it. He kicked it in the sides, and at a fierce gallop rode toward the Totten brothers and Maybelle. The girl stood helpless in his path. For a moment it seemed that boy and horse would be upon her. But in the fraction of time between reaching and not reaching her, Little Squire Jim veered the horse in a sharp wheel, swept by her, and was gone through the leaves of the mountainside. The action was so swift that the Totten men could only stand paralyzed, pitchforks drawn.

That night at the supper table Thag Totten said to his sister, "What you tryin to do today, Maybelle? Give Little Jim a fit?"

93

Maybelle blushed and ran from the table.

But the next afternoon she took great care with her chestnut hair. She brushed it to a gloss. She put on a dress with green ribbons. She went into the meadow with a bucket of water again. She waited under the tree.

Little Jim did not return that afternoon to the Totten meadow, nor did he any other afternoon that summer.

Nor did he return to plague Annie as she worked with her flowers. The trillium seeds fell and the leaves died back. The late summer flowers and the leaves withered, but never a shadow of Little Jim. "And me showin him my trillies in the spring," she complained.

"But you seed him smile. Nobody else seed him smile," Til said.

"But I shouldn't've spoke to him that way. I shouldn't've," she wailed. "And him no more'n a boy half-grown."

HARRIET

In the summer after Amelia Boyden's death, Dave Crockett, representing the school committee of which Thag Totten and Will Hollister were members, went to Tateboro to confer with the county superintendent about a teacher for the Cove school. He came back well pleased. The new teacher would be a young lady from Georgia, a Miss Harriet Evans. He had not seen her personally, but she was well spoken for, he said. Ellen Hull, a Tateboro matron in good standing, had been in school with her sister. Miss Evans, Dave said, had had a full year of college, and though young was eager to come up to the Cove to teach. Furthermore, he had suggested that she write the Hollisters about living with them for the winter. Clonda Hollister was pleased. And so, late in September Clonda and Will Hollister were on their porch when George Hull drove up into their yard and helped Harriet Evans out of his car.

Harriet was much younger than they had expected, and much prettier, with glowing complexion and gray-blue eyes. She was not tall even with her high heels, although she wore her bright auburn hair coiled into braids about her head to make her look taller, or perhaps older.

George helped Will Hollister carry the small trunk and boxes of books to the porch. Then they went back to the car. Will eyed it curiously. He had never had a car in his front yard before.

"Hard time comin up the mountain in that?" Will asked.

George smiled. "Once or twice I thought I'd have to send for a double muleteam."

"I reckon the goin back'll be easier than the comin up," Will said.

George glanced up to the sun. "I'd better be starting back now. I sure don't want to be caught on those curves in the night time."

"You're welcome to stay the night," Clonda invited.

George shook his head. "Take care of the little girl. She's not as old as she looks, but she's mighty smart with

96

children." And turning to Harriet, he added: "Write us, and when you can, come down to see us. Another pretty girl around the house suits me any day."

He crawled into his car and waved goodbye. When he had disappeared around the curve in the road, Clonda showed Harriet up to her room, and Will brought up the trunk and books.

"Hit'll be a warm room when the wind blows cold," Clonda said. "And the bed's thick with feathers to sleep on."

"I know I'll like it," Harriet answered. And then she smiled wistfully. "And thank you for letting me come to live with you for the winter."

"Hit's to our likin, too," Clonda answered. A wave of embarrassment swept over her. "Supper'll be ready close to sundown."

That night after supper Clonda said with sudden bravery, "And to think a girl what's been to a real college has set down and eat at my table, jest like folks."

"Oh, but I've just been one year."

"But hit were a real college?" Clonda asked, fear in her eyes.

"Oh, yes. And I'm going to teach a year or two and save, and then go back and finish."

Will, who had remained silent during most of the meal, said abruptly, "You're mighty young to be a school teacher."

"I'll be eighteen next month," Harriet answered, in confusion at his terse statement. "But I'm going to try to be a good teacher. I heard of the school up here from Ellen

Hull. And when I heard, I applied. I live in Georgia," she added, as if this bit of information would make things more nearly equal in some way.

Will's face was expressionless, but Clonda smiled encouragingly.

"And they told me to write you if I could live with you."

"Hit were nice, and we're mighty proud," Clonda said.

"Georgia's a mighty fer piece off," Will said.

"And you've been to a real college?" Clonda interrupted. "Maybe you could tell a body about goin to a real college and livin way off in Georgia."

"If you really want me to," Harriet answered, and under Clonda's encouragement she began talking. Will listened in silence, but Clonda's eyes were warm and enthusiastic. Finally, when it was near nine o'clock, Harriet said: "I think I'd better go up to bed. I want to go up to the school early in the morning."

Clonda lit a kerosene lamp and went ahead of her up the steps. When they were in the room, Clonda said, almost in a whisper, "Hit's more'n a body ken take in all at once."

"We'll have a whole winter," Harriet said.

Clonda looked quickly toward the door as if she were afraid someone might hear her admission. "I never even been over the mountain to Tateboro."

"Oh, but you must go with me sometime, when I go," Harriet answered.

"I reckon I'd like to drop dead first," Clonda said, and then she added wistfully, "But hit'll be good to think about when the snow gits to layin a long time on the fields." She had backed to the door. "I'll call you early in the mornin."

"Thank you so much," Harriet said. "I'm a little nervous about the first day, but I know—"

"Hit'll turn out all right," Clonda encouraged. "You jest git some sleep."

The next morning Harriet was up early, and after breakfast she walked the half-mile or more to the school.

The Cove schoolhouse sat on a protected hill on the road going toward Tateboro. Someone, sometime, had put a split-rail fence around the schoolyard. Just why, no one could tell. On a tall post in the yard was a great iron bell. A rope dangled from its handle in the stray winds of autumn and winter and summer and autumn again. The building had only one room, but it was tightly built; and for an unpainted frame building it had weathered the mountain storms with remarkable persistence. The pupils who attended the school with more or less mountain regularity ranged from the first grade to the sixth.

Harriet crossed the schoolyard and unlocked the door. Her first glance showed that she would have a great deal to do to get the room in order for the opening of school the next day, but she set to work with enthusiasm. She examined the supply of worn books. There were so few that she would have to bring her own books, she realized, to fill out. But she was undaunted, and the next day when the thirty or more pupils arrived, no one of them could tell that she felt nervous or hesitant. The first day passed in an emotion of excitement, but the next was easier, and at the end of the week she confessed to Clonda: "The children are so anxious to do everything I want, and so happy to learn. I'm glad every minute I came."

"A purty girl, tryin hard, ken do a lot of things,"

99

Clonda encouraged. "We've not had a school teacher that were young and purty in I don't know when."

"Oh, but I hope they don't do things for me just because—"

Clonda smiled. "Hit's yore ways, too, I reckon."

"But Mr. Hollister doesn't think—" Harriet did not finish.

Clonda patted her hand. "Don't you fret about Will. Hit's jest his way. He never was a man to feed all his hay at once."

"I'm going to try to be a good teacher," Harriet answered.

"Don't you fret about Will. You jest go on and teach yore school."

The first weeks of the school were busy. The routine of hearing lessons and getting the children well organized were happy days for Harriet. She wrote her friend, Ellen Hull, that every moment of her time was full and that there was little to disturb her happiness.

In the first week of October, however, when the early frost had set the maples and oaks aflame, Harriet looked away from her pupils and out the window. Across the road, among the trees, she thought she saw a horse and rider. She could not be sure; for the leaves and hair and horse seemed merged in a mass of red and brown and flaming orange. An hour later she passed the window. Still among the leaves was that suggestion of horse and rider. Harriet said nothing to her pupils, but at noon recess she went down to the fence close to the road. She examined the trees where she thought she had seen the horse and rider. There was nothing there.

The next day, however, the children were whispering excitedly when they came in from the noon recess. Harriet caught the words, "Little Squire Jim," and "He's wearin a shirt." She succeeded in quieting their whispering, but she noticed that it was hard for her to keep their attention on their lessons, and at the close of the school, when she gave the signal for dismissal, they virtually fled toward the door. Even Ancil Holt, whose week it was to stay and help tidy up the room, was uncertain in obedience.

"What's the matter with the children?" she asked. "You've not been like yourselves all afternoon."

Ancil looked toward the door. "Hit's Little Squire Jim."

"Little Squire Jim?"

"He's under the tree waitin."

"But what's that to do with us?" Harriet asked.

"He's aimin to ride right up in the school. Right in this room."

"Oh, that couldn't be," Harriet answered with a touch of irritation. "Who ever heard of people riding horses in a house?"

"Little Squire will, ef it suits him," Ancil answered, edging toward the door with frightened eyes. "And that hoss of hissen. Hits feet'll tear up the whole schoolhouse." He edged still nearer the door. "Hit rode up in the Campbells' house, right in the dinin room, and eat a whole sugar pie right off the dinner table."

"The horse?"

Ancil nodded.

She smiled. "You may go."

Ancil did not wait for a second invitation.

That night Harriet ate her supper in silence. At first

101

she thought she would tell the Hollisters about the absurd story of the children, and then she hesitated. What if it were only some joke the pupils were playing on her? The thought made her more unhappy as she reflected on how cordial they had been to her at first. She went up to her room immediately after supper. In the security of her room she felt calmer. Perhaps it was a joke, and if it were a joke, it would be over the next day. The thought eased her and she prepared for bed.

The next morning, however, a third of her pupils were absent, and those present kept glancing surreptitiously toward the door. Harriet pretended that she saw nothing. At noon recess she sent them out as usual, but when she had eaten her own lunch she became conscious that the sounds from outside had suddenly ended. She went to the door. The children were huddled around the bell-post, their eyes on the trees across the road, but before she could call, or make some move, the horse and rider broke from the leaves and with flying leap cleared the fence and galloped toward the bell. The children scattered.

Little Jim slid off the horse, dropped the rein. Instinctively Harriet backed into the room and down the aisle to a position behind her desk. With the desk in front of her she felt safer. Her heart was beating. In a moment he was in the door. She had the feeling that she was in the presence of something wild and strange and uncontrollable. But something inside rose to make her say, "I'm Miss Harriet Evans." Her voice sounded bodiless and far-away.

"Proud to know you." He had stopped halfway down the aisle.

"You'll want a desk. That one," she heard herself saying, 'over there."

He turned.

"The biggest one in the back, with the green book on it."

In a kind of confused amazement she realized that he was obeying her, was going over to the desk and slipping into it. The desk was too small. His chest and shoulders and head loomed above it. "How enormous he is," she thought in a sudden wave of panic. For the moment he seemed too big for the room even. She put her hand on her desk to steady herself.

"Is the desk too small?" she asked stupidly.

He did not answer. There was nothing in his face to suggest that he had even heard her.

"I don't know why the other children haven't come back in," she heard herself saying, and before she realized what she was doing she was going down the aisle toward the door. The movement gave her a sense of control. She glanced toward him. He was following her with his eyes. For a moment she felt like running, but when she reached the door she saw the stallion at the bell-post outside. Its ears were pointed toward the school door; its eyes were watchful and bright. There was no sense of wildness about the horse; rather there was a calm patience. She thought of the boy seated inside. "Why, he's just a boy come to my school," she said aloud. "And this is just his way." The desire to flee suddenly left her, and she looked about the yard for the children. She called. There was no answer. She went into the yard. On the far side of the fence she saw a head. Then others. She called to them, asked them to come back into the school. Uncertainly they responded, but they made a wide detour around the horse at the bell-post. "Don't be silly," she encouraged. "Little Jim's just come to school. See, his horse is there. And he's not hurting anything."

She got them into a group, and then at their head she led them back into the room. She told them to take their seats. Pale and hesitantly they did so, all of them, that is, except Arabel Leach. She stood back against the wall. On her pale face the freckles stood out like bronze specks.

"Take your seat, Arabel," Harriet said as quietly as she could.

Arabel shook her head in desperation. She was thirteen and her rusty-brown plaits bobbed against the wall.

"Do as I say," Harriet commanded.

With an expression in her eyes as if she had been ordered to go into the maw of terror, she slipped into the vacant desk in front of Little Jim. The other children watched with wide eyes.

"Now, all of you open your books and begin studying."

With the movement of automatons, they did as she commanded. Then, with all the calmness she could muster, she called a group to her desk for lessons, and when that was done she moved about the room supervising the studying, talking quietly to them as if nothing were different. When she felt that the tension had eased, and by her watch she knew that she was in the last hour of the school day, she looked toward Little Jim. He was turning the pages of the book which he had found on the desk. Nothing about him suggested that he was aware of the effect of his

104

presence in the room. He apparently was in a world of his own. His feet were sprawled in the aisle on each side of the desk, his mass of red curling hair bent over the book. He was turning the pages in vague detachment. She asked him to come to her desk and bring the book with him.

He made no move to obey her.

She asked him again. He only continued to turn the pages. There was not the slightest move on his part to suggest that he meant to obey her. Her impulse was to ask him again, but then she grew afraid. To cover her fear she opened a book on her desk to make it seem that his lack of response was of small importance. But an abnormal silence had fallen over the room. For a long time she did not look up from her desk. When she did, Little Jim's gaze was full on her. She looked back down at her book. In a few minutes she looked up again. He was still staring at her. Frantically she glanced at her watch. It was too early, but she would do it. She stood up. The children, not waiting for her word of dismissal, sprang up, and in no more than a moment, it seemed to Harriet, they had fled the room, and no one was there except herself and Little Jim. He too had risen and was coming up the aisle toward her.

"What's your name?" She tried to seize the initiative.

"Jim Boyden."

The words were the first he had uttered since that 'Proud to know you' of almost two hours before.

"You and I ought to get along well together," she tried to say in a steady voice. "We've both got red hair. And I love horses too. I like to ride."

He stopped, his eyes on the braids about her head. The afternoon sun through the window had turned them into bright copper.

"And you plan to come to my school?" she asked.

His gaze dropped from her hair to her face.

"If you're coming to my school, you'll have to do as I ask."

His gaze swept back to her hair. His hands moved, but he made no answer.

"Then I'll have to go home," she said abruptly, and she closed the book on her desk.

"I'm much obliged," he said, and with no more than that he turned and went down the aisle. In a moment he was out the door, and through the window she caught a glimpse of the wheeling horse, heard the clatter of hoofs losing themselves down the road, and she realized that he was gone.

She sank into her chair. She was trembling. "I must hurry home," she thought; "he'll come back." And before she could calm herself, she was getting her coat. She locked the door and, half-walking and half-running, she went toward home.

That night at supper she told the Hollisters of the events of the day. They were surprised.

"I never heared of a Boyden wantin to come to a school with folks," Clonda burst out.

"But he was there," Harriet said, "in a yellow-and-gray checked shirt. It seems like a dream while I'm telling you, but he was there. Right in the room."

"In a yellow checked shirt?" Clonda asked.

Harriet nodded.

106

"Big enough to wear his daddy's shirts already. Never saw the Big Squire without a gray-and-yellow checked shirt, in all my days. The Old Lady Boyden, I hear tell, dyed the wool, made the cloth, and sewed the shirts jest to the Big Squire's size. Must've made enough fer the Big Squire to last the Little Squire till the day he's old enough to git killed."

"But what kind of a boy is he?" Harriet cried.

They tried to explain Little Jim to her. They tried to explain his father, and his grandfather, and the ways of the Boydens.

"But hasn't his aunt, Mrs. Gwynn, done anything for him since his mother died?"

They shook their heads. "Never hear tell of her since the day of Amelia Boyden's buryin," Clonda said.

"Reckon she figures he's gonna git killed in his own way," Will said.

"But that's silly," Harriet burst out. "People don't have to fulfill something like that. I mean just getting killed, just because—" she broke off. Will was scowling at her.

"Hit's the way of the Boyden men," he said.

"But Little Jim's not a man," Harriet cried. "He's just a boy. There he sat today, looking at pictures in a book, like any boy."

"What kind of a shirt did you say he were wearin?" Will asked tersely.

"A gray-and-yellow checked one."

"Were it too big for him?" Clonda whispered.

"Not much," Harriet said. "Why?"

Clonda looked at Will. "Annie Umbarger's always sayin the Big Squire aint layin in that grave like folks say."

"I aint agreein to everything Annie Umbarger says," Will answered stubbornly.

"But what will I do with him?" Harriet asked. "He's there in the room."

"Do nothin," Clonda said. "Jest do nothin. Nobody ken do anything with the Little Squire except maybe Dave Crockett and—" she paused; "and maybe Annie Umbarger."

"But what if he comes back to school tomorrow?"

Clonda reached over and patted her hand. "Little Squire's never come the same place twice, cept to Annie's and to Dave Crockett's."

However, the next morning, when Harriet arrived, Little Jim and his horse were in the yard by the bell. He was again wearing the yellow-and-gray checked shirt, and he had made some attempt at combing his hair. He sat motionless on his horse when she passed him, as if he did not see her, but when she gave the signal for the opening of school, he was the first to enter. He went directly to his seat. Harriet began the routine of the day as if he were not in the room. She went about hearing the lessons. As the morning advanced a growing sense of panic crept over her. The things the Hollisters had told her took possession of her. Every time she glanced in his direction, she found him staring at her. She dared not go near him or speak to him, but she was conscious that he followed her every move, every gesture of her head, and the enormousness of his shoulders and head above the desk began to grow more ominous in her thoughts. To quiet her fears she tried to act as if he were not there. But he would not be ignored. He arose and started walking toward the desk. A tense

108

silence fell over the room. Frantically Harriet gathered a half-dozen books and thrust them out to him.

"I'm much obliged," he said, taking them and going back to his seat.

In a moment he began turning the pages. All day he turned the pages. The next morning before school she put a stack of books on his desk, and the next morning, a new stack. For days he did nothing but turn pages of the books which she placed each morning on his desk.

The second week Harriet impulsively asked him if he would do her a favor. Would he raise the window for her?

"It would pleasure me," he said simply.

After that she began asking little favors of him. Would he care to shift her desk? Would he like to ring the bell for her in the mornings and at recess times? She multiplied her requests.

He did everything she asked of him simply and with an air of great courtesy. And the simplicity with which he moved and did these things began to break down the air of abnormal tension in the room. Even the children began to relax, and she herself began to lose her sense of uneasiness.

The third week, however, he refused to go out at recess with the children. He wanted to stay in the room, turning the pages of the books and, more often than she wished, staring at her hair. The old uneasiness swept over her. "I wonder if you wouldn't like to watch the boys at recess and not let them fight each other," she asked.

"A man's goin to fight, if he's goin to fight," he objected.

"But I don't want fighting at recess time," she insisted.

He got up, closed his book, and went outside. After re-

109

cess he came back to his desk, not turning the leaves of the books, only staring at her.

In desperation Harriet went to see Annie Umbarger.

"I don't know what I'll do with him," she cried helplessly to Annie. "He'll seem to be reading. But I never know. I gave him a *Robinson Crusoe,* and every day he turns the pages. Every day. And he won't take any other book now. That's the only book he'll even pretend to read any more, although he must have gone through it twenty times already. Finally I just wrote his name in it and gave it to him, and told him to read it at home. And the next day he came back to school without it. And now he sits there looking at me. That's all he does. All day. Just looks at me. I don't know what to do."

"His maw was a readin woman. And maybe he reads more'n you think. But I'd not cross him, ef I was you," Annie cautioned.

"But I'm not afraid of him any more," Harriet insisted. "Except there's something strange in the way he looks at me."

"Jest pay no attention to him," Annie repeated.

"I've tried that, too, and then after school he waits on his horse in the yard, and follows behind me until I get home. I don't know what to do."

Annie's eyes narrowed. "You heared me," she warned.

The next day Harriet tried to follow Annie's advice. She asked no favors of him. She tried to pretend that he was not in the room. But that afternoon, after she had locked up the school and was far down the road, she knew he was behind her. She slowed up, she loitered, half-hoping he would catch up with her. She did not know what she would have said or done if he had. But he did not come closer. The next day, in spite of herself, her glance strayed more often than she wished to his strange face and somber eyes. Sometimes she thought his face was that of a boy. Then, that of a grown man. Sometimes she was startled to see his eyes turn into a vague blackness. Then she grew afraid and hurriedly called a class of spellers or readers about her and tried to ignore him completely.

The pupils began to sense a renewed tension in the room, but with determination they kept their eyes riveted on their books; even on the day when Little Jim got up and began walking restlessly in the back of the room, they bent their heads closer over their books.

Several times he went out and looked at the bell in the yard, as if he would be ringing it. He came back to his desk and kept his eyes on Harriet until she should give the signal by nodding her head. But she kept busy with the others, never raising her eyes above the nearest pupils. He got up and went out again. His restlessness communicated itself to his horse, for after he had come to take his seat again with sullen deliberateness, the horse violated the dropped reins and trotted by outside the windows, rattling the stones with its hoofs. Little Jim went outside, and, catching the horse, dropped the rein over the bell-post. When he took his seat again, the eyes of the children were still on their books. Harriet began explaining for the fourth or fifth time a simple problem to an outwardly attentive little boy. Suddenly the tension was broken by Arabel Leach's cry, "Stop! You're hurtin me. You're hurtin me!"

Frightened eyes of the children turned toward Arabel.

She was trying to rearrange her hair—brown with the streaks of copper red in its thin braids. "He's puttin his hand on my hair. He's puttin his hand on my hair."

Harriet stood up behind her desk. She was pale, but there was anger in her voice. "Jim Boyden," she said, "I'll . . . I'll . . . I'll keep you in after school if you touch Arabel's hair again."

Even before the pause at the end of her words, even before she could draw breath for another threat, Jim reached over and caught Arabel's hair in his hand and jerked with such fierceness that the girl shrieked in terror and pain.

The children nearest Arabel fell out of their seats and ran stumbling and crying toward Harriet's desk. She put her hands on the nearest ones and pushed their faces against her dress to quiet their cries.

Little Jim rose slowly out of his desk and stalked from the room.

Quickly Harriet commanded the children to get back to their seats and to open their books. She herself went to the rear door, and, placing her back against it, talked to them in as calm a voice as she could muster. Soon they grew quiet; but at the noon recess the younger ones pleaded to stay in. A few of the older ones went out. When they returned, she caught fragments of their whisperings, "He's gone . . . He's nowhere around. . . ."

However, at the end of the school day Little Jim was sitting on his horse outside. She could do nothing but urge the older children to take the younger and hurry out the door to the side. She did not think of fleeing herself. When the last pupil had gone, she saw Little Jim slide off the horse, and, when he was outside the door, she said, "Sit down, Jim."

He came up the aisle and took a seat near her desk.

"Jim," she said, as if the situation were the most natural in the world, "why did you jerk Arabel's hair that way when I asked you not to?"

He moved his fingers over the top of the desk caressingly. "So you'd make me stay in," he said slowly.

"But you put your hands on Arabel's hair before that."

His fingers continued to move softly over the desk top.

"Why?" she pursued.

"Her hair's a little like yours when you stand in the sun."

Harriet flushed.

"You mustn't talk that way, Jim. I can't let you come to my school if you talk like that." And then a nervous strength rising in her made her add: "I don't see why you came to school anyhow. You won't read or try to do anything. You just sit. Why do you come to school, anyhow?"

His hands still moved on the desk caressingly. Something in his face seemed about to break through, like a faint smile trembling upon a knife edge. "To ring the bell for you."

"But that's no reason," she answered. "I could get somebody else to do that. Anybody."

The hands on the desk stopped moving. The suggestion of a smile disappeared. There was only the look of a boy, hurt, in his face. He rose. "I reckon you better get somebody else, then."

Before she could answer, he was gone.

113

The next morning he was not at the door. Nor was he the next day, or the next.

"But I didn't mean to hurt his feelings," Harriet wailed to Annie Umbarger in her kitchen. "I can still see that hurt look in his face. I want to tell him I'm sorry."

"No." And Annie's eyes gleamed. "How you know his daddy aint settin up there in that house this minute tellin him what to do?"

"But his father's dead," Harriet tried to answer.

Annie's eyes burned deeper. "I aint never seen him buried. Nobody's seen him buried I ever heared tell of. Hit wouldn't faze me one minute to see him come ridin out of that valley on that black hoss of hissen any night when the lightnin's flarin the sky."

"But—"

"Little Jim's jest like his daddy, I tell you. He's not natural. You jest let him stay up there in that valley till it suits him to come out. He'll come out some day and never be no different. Last April time I flew at him fer settin in my flowers like some October mountain thing. And I didn't see hoof nor hide of him fer too long to count. And then jest yestiddy . . ."

"But I dream about him at night. I want to tell him I'm sorry."

Annie narrowed her eyes. "Hit don't do a girl good to be dreamin about a boy, and that boy a good-lookin boy." She nodded her sharp face, eyes glinting. "He's his daddy." She paused. "You hear what I'm sayin? His daddy and his grandaddy and his daddy before him. An don't say I never breshed yore ear with a warnin stick, a-knowin what I know. He's a Boyden man."

Harriet blushed. "But he's just a boy, I tell you—"

"Well, I've seed what I've seed," Annie argued. "And you're young and pretty like a shade-flower—"

"But what is it you've seen?" Harriet cried.

"I've seen Little Squire Jim lookin yestiddy behind my hawthorn bush, and it no more'n come November—"

"But what was he looking for?"

Annie's eyes were still warning. A glint of a smile was in them. "I aint tellin everything I know. But don't never say I aint breshed yore ear in passin with a warnin. And hit jest November. . . ."

When Little Jim did not return the next week, or the next, Harriet found herself walking home from school looking hopefully for him among the trees along the road, or suddenly turning around, expecting to find him following her. "I just want to tell him I'm sorry I hurt his feelings," she cried to herself. One day she even went to the road that led into Little Stepper Valley. She examined the boulders that marked the entrance, wondering what lay inside the hills, wondering what she would do if Little Jim should suddenly ride up on his horse and ask her to ride into that valley. "I'd go just to see what's in there," she said to herself. "I wouldn't be afraid. He's just a boy. He's not the way everybody says he is. He didn't mean to hurt Arabel Leach. I made him hurt her by saying what I did." She took a few steps through the rocks. The sudden thickness of the trees along the road made her stop. Annie Umbarger's warning, 'He's a Boyden man and the Big Squire's a-layin up there in that house not buried and roamin the mountains on a black hoss,' made her fall back with beating heart. "I'm not afraid of Little Jim," she tried

115

to tell herself. "It's the things I don't know that make my heart go this way."

But the afternoon when Harriet turned from locking the school door and saw Little Jim actually sitting on his horse outside the gate, she could not be sure of anything. She saw him slide off the horse and wait at its head near the gate. Going toward him, she cried, "Why Jim, where have you been? You haven't been back to school, and—"

"I've got four little foxes," he said.

"Foxes? Four little foxes?"

"And one of them's for you."

She glanced down at his empty hands.

"You can ride Eldo," he said.

She looked in his face again to be sure of his meaning.

"You can ride Eldo," he repeated.

"But, Jim," she said, to cover her confusion. "Foxes aren't little in the fall. Foxes are little in the spring."

"And one of them's for you."

The insistence of his words was mingled with pleading. She had never thought of Little Jim pleading for anything.

"All of them's for you, if you want," he added wistfully.

He looked so like a boy, so like the boy who had risen with hurt eyes from his desk with 'I reckon you better get somebody else, then,' that she said impulsively, "I'll have to change first."

He walked behind her toward the Hollister house, leading the horse by the bridle. When she came to the last curve in the road before coming in sight of the Hollister house, she said, "You wait here." And then she added, "I don't think I ought to go, Jim."

116

She hurried toward the house.

When she came out again he motioned her to mount the horse. She held back. She felt a moment of fear at the prospect of mounting the stallion, recalling all that she had heard of its wildness. He held the horse's head. It stood motionless. She mounted. Then they started, he holding his hand on the bridle and jogging along in front. Soon they passed through the two boulders at the entrance, and, walking or trotting, went deep into the Valley before turning off through the trees. As the trees grew heavy and thicker, uneasiness began to stir within her, to creep up into thwarted admissions. Yet with this uneasiness she also felt a sense of security as she watched the easy movement of his shoulders and body as he led the horse over the rocks. The rhythm of his muscles, the swift direction of his path lulled her and swept her on.

They passed into a tangle of leafless bushes and trees, through a cluster of spruces so thick and dark they tore at her in passing, up a rocky incline. Suddenly before them was an entrance into the mountainside, covered by logs and skins.

He waited for her to dismount. She hesitated. The horse tossed its head. Finally she slipped off, and following him under the skins, she found herself in a rocky cave. Vaguely, from the pale light that broke through a crevice above, she discerned a rough bed of hewn logs. Furs and skins of animals lay over the bed and hung from the rocks about it. In a high niche a candle burned under a crucifix, and near it in the glow of the flame was a copper luster pitcher. Near the rude furnace was a blackened copper kettle. Her eyes

117

went back to the luster pitcher near the flame. He followed her glance.

"It's like your hair in the sun," he said.

The shadows in the deep rocks grew suddenly ragged. Fears she had forced back stirred, but he was so intent on his purpose that she was swept on. He was pointing to a corner. Impelled, she moved toward it. Under jagged niches in a nest was a mother fox, lying on its side, its head raised, its ears alert. At breast were four little foxes, suckling. They burrowed with spasmodic thrusts into the breast as the vixen lay motionless, nose sharp to a wet point, eyes gleaming and wary on the two figures looking down upon it.

"I never saw a little fox before," Harriet breathed. "Do they bite?"

He reached down and picked one up. The eyes of the vixen followed it. He placed it in her hands.

"Hold it," he said.

It was no larger than a kitten; its fur, soft and glossy, was bright-red. Its eyes, not long open, were dark beads. Its nose was sharp and cool. She seated herself on the edge of the cot. She stroked its fur, then held it over her breast as she would a baby. So rapt was she that she was only vaguely conscious that Little Jim was drawing near her in the shadows, so near he was beginning to close out the light, and so close she could feel the warmth of his body, his quickened breathing. Something drew her eyes up to his shoulders, to his half-opened mouth, and to the encompassing blackness of his eyes. Inside her the fears which she had held buried swiftly uncoiled themselves and fused with the memory of the play of his muscles coming over

118

the hill. Suddenly she felt that she was in a kind of dream with a living, breathing, pulsing being closing about her. In terror she felt spasmodic biting at her fingers from the squeezed little thing in her hands, heard, as if afar off, its strangled yelp, and in the flame of the moment she dropped the thing and, running toward the doorway, fought through the skins to the outside, stumbling, running, half-falling, pushing limbs and twigs from her face and hair, trying somehow to retrace the way she had come. She ran on wildly until she came to an open meadow. Then behind her she heard the pound of horse's hoofs, and she was conscious of the horse with the boy upon it flashing by in the openness of the meadow. She stopped. Ahead of her the boy and the horse had drawn to a halt. He slipped off. He dropped the rein over the horse's head. He ran to one side, away from the horse, crying to her: "Ride to the sun. Ride to the sun."

Impelled by his words, she ran toward the horse. She took the rein and led it to the log and clambered on.

"Ride to the sun. Ride to the sun," she heard him cry again.

But she was too excited to do more than kick her heels into the sides of the horse. The sudden burst of speed was frightening. She found herself desperately holding on to the horse's mane, not caring what direction it took. To get away was all she wanted. The horse pounded through the trees, following a kind of path. She let it take its own way.

Soon the horse came out into open fields, and suddenly looming up before her she saw a massive brick house. "Little Stepper House" flashed through her mind. "The horse has galloped home." And with the realization of where she was came also Annie's warning: 'The Big Squire's settin up there in that house dead and ready to come ridin out of the Valley.' The sun, she now realized, was not ahead of her, but at her back, had been at her back all the time, and she had been too terrified to know it. Impulsively she tugged at the reins to turn the horse's head. It wheeled at her direction. The sun struck her in the face. She leaned farther over the mane and urged the horse forward. Away from the house and down the road the horse sped. Ahead of her through the cutting branches she could see Hanging Rock. A sense of safety surged up inside her at its sight.

The road grew more open. Hanging Rock was drawing nearer. She urged the horse on. She reached a crest. Suddenly, through the trees and to the left of her, she thought she saw the flash of a figure, moving with satyr-like swiftness. But she could not be sure. She reached another crest. Before her was Cove Road. Impulsively she tugged at the reins. The horse slowed. She tugged again. The horse slowed still more. Amazed at its response to her will, she pulled it sharply. The horse came to a full stop. She looked over her shoulder.

Back of her the gaunt trees were thick and dark. Yet in their gaunt darkness she was sure she saw Little Jim. He was standing motionless, his feet wide apart, his hands hanging down. The sun's rays caught his hair into a red mass. Impulsively she waved.

Then she dashed down the road.

At the Hollister gate she slid off the horse and dropped the rein over the gatepost.

The November sun set. Darkness crept out of the trees. The horse tossed its head at the gate. Finally she led it to the stable, fed it, and dropped the latch on the door.

The next morning when she went out the horse was gone.

The November days were rainy and Blue Snake River ran full, but the early December days were cold and dry. In a corner room, which served as a kind of office, Dave Crockett kept a wood fire going, and from time to time when his hands grew stiff he would push up the sluice lever, stop the ponderous turning of the grindstones, and go in to warm his hands. But not often. He was thinking of Little Squire Jim and the words of Til Umbarger. Til would not say how he knew, but he intimated that Little Jim was living in a cave back in the Valley, "and maybe eatin raw meat like some wild animal." Dave was troubled. "Hit's no way fer a boy to live, even ef he were the Little Squire," he grumbled.

From outside, through the rumble of cogs and grinding stones, he heard the rattle of the engine of a truck. Not often had an automobile come into the Cove in the wintertime. He pushed up the sluice lever and went to the office door. A man was climbing out of a Ford truck. He was a slight man with a battered felt hat, and his overcoat lapels were pulled over his chest. He came into Dave's office and went toward the stove.

"Cold weather we're having," he remarked, holding his hands before the stove. "Buying up old furniture. Run a second-hand place in Tateboro. Been there fifteen years." He pulled out a soiled card and handed it to Dave. "Ephram J. Caskey is the name. Buy anything. Any old kitchen tables, drop-leaf, or spinning wheels, or junk you want to get rid of?"

Dave shook his head. "Reckon not. Savin everything to set up my grandaughter to housekeepin sometime, ef she needs it."

Ephram turned back to warm his hands again. As he did so, he caught sight of a chair at Dave's work table. The seat was showing wear, but Ephram's quick eyes noticed the beadwork of brass around the seat and the lightness of the design of the chair. Ephram moved closer. His eyes ran over the delicate inlay of white in the oval back. He put out his hand to touch it. He sensed the strength of its construction. "It's a Hepplewhite and a master chair to a set, if I ever set my eyes on one," he thought. His hands trembled at the realization, but lest the trembling betray him, he put his hands in his overcoat pockets. He moved back with elaborate casualness to the stove.

"Where'd you get a chair like that?"

"Little Squire Jim give it to me."

"Got any more like it?"

"No."

Ephram looked about the office generally and said in an offhand manner, "I don't suppose you'd want to sell it."

"No."

"I'll give you three dollars for it, if you'll throw in two pecks of cornmeal to boot. The meal's worth more than the chair."

"The Little Squire give it to me."

"I know. I heard you say that before. But—"

"Wouldn't part with it fer hits weight in gold."

Ephram turned back to the stove. "I'll take the meal anyhow."

When Dave brought the meal Ephram asked, "Who'd you say gave it to you?"

"Little Squire."

"Who's he?"

"He's the Big Squire's boy from over in Little Stepper," and Dave gestured toward the Valley.

Ephram's eyes narrowed. "Kin folks of Old Lady Gwynn?"

"That's one way of sayin it, I reckon," Dave answered.

"In some kind of shooting scrape over a woman outside Tateboro ten or more years back?"

"That were Little Squire's daddy."

"How'd he make out? Never heard of him since."

"He were killed."

"Never heard that."

"They fetched him back in a box," said Dave.

"As I recollect, he killed the woman's husband."

"The Big Squire were killed," Dave said, and went toward the door. The matter was closed. "Reckon I'd better be gettin back to my grindin."

Ephram turned toward the stove. "Don't want to sell that chair?"

Dave did not answer.

"How'd you get into that valley from this side?" Ephram asked.

"Two big rocks down the road you come up. But the Little Squire's invitin no man to come into the Valley."

123

"Not planning to go," Ephram answered. "Just asked in passing." He sensed Dave's antagonism. But he had met that before in his business. However, he moved generally toward the door. "I'll stop by again when I'm passing. Maybe next time you'll sell that chair. Not worth more'n a dollar or two, but I'll give you ten dollars for it."

"Little Squire give it to me," Dave said patiently.

Ephram buttoned his coat and went out.

He crawled into his truck. "Reckon I'll go back the way I came," he shouted over the engine's noise.

Turning the truck around, he headed back as if he were going to Tateboro, but when he passed the first curve he kept his eyes alert for the two boulders, and when he came to them he turned in. The road was at first easy enough, but soon it grew almost impassable. Ephram tied ropes around the wheels to help the chains. Twice he had to get out to remove dead limbs from the road. But he drove on. "If the fellow has the other chairs and table and sideboard to match that chair, it'll be worth it. Museum pieces," he kept telling himself. And as he careened on he planned in his mind how he would approach the matter. "I'll get him to let me look around. Then I'll get him to talk. I'll get one piece at a time from him, and then offer him something for the rest of the stuff as a favor." The truck bogged down again. He got out and put rough stones under the wheels. Then he dumped the cornmeal into the mud and used the sack for a tread. The truck pulled out.

At last, behind the leafless trees, Little Stepper House loomed up in the dusk ahead of him. Ephram drove his truck to the side and turned it around. "So it'll be easy to

124

put the stuff in," he said to himself. He looked about the house. It seemed more enormous when he stood close to it. The front was dark and bare. Except for the open windows of one upstairs room in the corner, the house looked lifeless. He decided to go around to the back. The back door to the kitchen stood open and in the doorway he saw a figure. For a moment Ephram hesitated. A light from inside outlined the shoulders and head. They seemed to fill the doorway, yet the figure was not tall.

"The old man at the mill said for me to come to see you," Ephram said.

The dark eyes seemed to search through the dusk. Then the figure dropped back. "Come in."

Ephram entered. The room was unlighted except for a wood fire and a candle, flickering red under a crucifix in the far corner. Vaguely Ephram made out two heavy hutch tables. Both were piled with china and metal utensils, copper and brass, and mounds of clothing in disarray. In the fireplace were an iron crane and a spit. On the mantel above were a few cups and odd pitchers. "Copper luster and handleless cups. And pewter plates," Ephram gasped. He turned halfway about, his eyes more accustomed to the half-lit room. Against the wall to the side was a piece of furniture such as he had never expected to see. It was of dark wood. "A wig stand, if I ever saw one." He turned back to the luster cups on the mantel.

"Sit."

In his excitement Ephram had forgotten Jim. He saw him now, closer to the fire. "Why, he's just a boy," Ephram muttered to himself. Aloud he said: "I can't stay long. And

125

I'll tell you why I'm here. The old man at the mill said for me to come in here. And he said to ask you to show me around."

Jim's eyes were dark on him. "Old Dave Crockett say that?"

"Yes."

"What you want to see?" Jim's eyes still searched his face.

"A room or two." And Ephram waved generally toward the front of the house. "The old man—"

"If Old Dave asked me to, I'm mighty proud to favor him," Jim said, and, going to the wig stand, he lit a lamp.

He led the way into a dark hall. In the half-light Ephram could see a great staircase that curved up to the second floor. Jim turned to a pair of high double-doors. A key was in the lock of one of them. He turned it, and the door swung heavily back. Jim held the lamp high over his head. Its rays picked in shadowy detail a long, dim room lined with portraits, and filled with furnishings once elegant and rich. A crystal chandelier with wilted candles hung from the high ceiling. The windows were heavily draped. At the sight of them Ephram caught his breath. "They're brocatelle overhangings and gold-leaf valences, if I ever saw any," he muttered, and his eyes traveled with avid speed over the rest of the room. Near him was a carved settee, upholstered in faded gold damask. At its side, on a delicately carved table with turned edges, a few dusty books and small bejeweled box. On a larger table between two windows was an elaborately branched silver candelabra, tarnished almost to a black, and about its base were pieces of dusty procelain. "God," Ephram breathed. "What

126

ı find! And I'll get it all from him." He caught himself up. He did not want the boy to notice his excitement.

To throw him off, Ephram turned his eyes back to the portraits along the walls. He gestured toward the two at the far end of the room, over the mantel—one of a woman in elaborate flowered silk, her hair piled high in a powdered pompadour, the other of a man in a wig, his lace-cuffed hand on a sword hilt. The face under the wig seemed vaguely familiar in some far-off associative way. Ephram felt that he had seen it in some history book once as a child. "Whose picture is that over the mantel?" he asked abruptly, pointing.

"Grandpa Jim."

"And that?" Ephram continued, pointing to one on the near wall.

Jim put the lamp on the table and went closer. Then he backed away and stood with his hands behind him, his feet together, as would a boy whose mother has asked him to stand up straight when he spoke. "Grandpa Jim. Killed fightin redcoats."

"And that one next to it?"

"Grandpa Jim. Killed in a shootin fight over a mountain woman." He ran his hands through his hair in sudden effort to remember.

Ephram paused. He wondered if it were time to come around to the furniture. He decided to wait a little longer. "Who's that one?" he said, pointing to a dull portrait of a man in a later dress than any of the others.

"Grandpa Jim. He was a cussin man and a ridin man." A note of enthusiasm crept into his voice. "He took hold of a streak of lightnin, I hear folks say, and if the wind's

127

right folks can hear him cussin and ridin in the night time. I never heard him," he finished simply.

"How many of your grandfathers been killed?"

Without moving other than to raise his hand the boy pointed to the one over the mantel, then to another, and rapidly skipping over a tawny-haired figure in a dull frame, he went on to another, and then to another. "All of them." He paused. Then he added, "And I'm just bidin my time."

Ephram went close to the dull portrait the boy had passed over. There was something strikingly familiar about the lean face, the deep-set eyes, the tawny hair. He looked closer. There was no mistaking the face.

"One of your folks?"

"Grandpa Jim knows him. He's a law man and can hit a bear in the eye a mile off with a gun, my pa says." He ran his hand through his hair again impulsively. "I'm aimin to ride over the mountain and get him to touch up a paper, come spring time, if I know which way to ride. Before I'm killed."

"But that's Andrew Jackson, isn't it?" Ephram burst out.

Jim turned swiftly. "You know him?"

"But he's been—" Ephram swallowed the word *dead* in his throat. The eyes of the boy were on him, dark and questioning. The dim shadows of the room crept about them. For a moment nothing was real, this room with the fading portraits, the dust on things a hundred years old, two hundred years old.

"And so you're going to get this man Jackson to touch up a paper?" Ephram heard himself asking.

128

"Come spring time."

Ephram held his flashlight hard to make sure of his sense. The switch under his finger slipped. The beam lit up a corner of the ceiling. Automatically he asked: "What happened to your own pa? Did he get killed, or did he kill that man? Where's he now? Upstairs?"

Swiftly, so swiftly that Ephram could hardly realize the change, Jim was at the table and had lifted the lamp. "I've got to feed my horse," he said.

Ephram gasped. He had not been prepared for such a swift turn of the boy's mood. "Wait a minute," he called. "I want to buy some of this old stuff. Give you—"

"Boydens don't sell their things."

"But—"

"Boydens don't sell their things." Jim was at the door now, his eyes black and insistent. Ephram found himself following helplessly out of the room. But once in the hall ahead of the boy, he recovered himself, and, turning his flashlight through the door into the room across the hall, he pushed in a foot. The flashlight picked out a jumble of chairs and table and dining furnishings. The light struck the mates to the Hepplewhite chair in Dave Crockett's mill, and the sideboard. He tried to go into the room, but Jim stepped in front of him, blocking his light, pushing him back into the hall.

"Then if you won't sell anything from in there, what've you got upstairs?" Ephram persisted. "Any old tester-beds with curtains? Give you top price."

But Jim held the lamp into his face, forcing him back. "Didn't you hear me say I've got to feed my horse?"

Ephram stumbled. His flashlight fell on the floor and

rolled along the hall until it was stopped by a table. Ephram knelt to retrieve it. He saw the pedestal with its claw feet, its lyre of brass strings.

"I'll give you twenty-five dollars for this little table," he said desperately.

"Boydens don't sell their things."

"I'll give you fifty."

"Boydens don't sell their things."

"A hundred then." Ephram looked up. In the weird, distorted light of the lamp he saw Jim's face over him, pale in fury. Ephram tried to rise, but his knees wouldn't move. "I never meant harm," he tried to say, but his words jumbled themselves. The face moved away. Ephram reached for his flashlight again. His panic lessened. He stood up. The boy was in the kitchen. "He'll come around," he said aloud, "if I keep after him." Swiftly he turned the flashlight on the table and knelt to examine the pedestal. "It's a Duncan Phyfe sewing table," he muttered. "I could get a thousand for it. Maybe two thousand," and turning his head he shouted, loud enough for the boy in the kitchen to hear him. "I'll give you a hundred and fifty dollars for this little table."

His voice filled the hall, but before he could shout again Ephram found himself caught and lifted into the air. His voice strangled in his throat. His hands and feet struggled wildly. He tried to cry out. He tried to grasp at the door frame leading into the kitchen, at the door frame leading outside. He clutched at the night air. He screamed. His voice sounded thin and strangled in his throat. He found himself on the ground.

"Go on home off my land."

Running and stumbling Ephram reached his truck and started the engine. Vaguely he was aware of the boy standing under a tree watching him. He headed down the yard toward the road. He was too terrified to turn to see if he were being followed.

When the truck had sputtered down the road, the silence of the Valley fell around Little Stepper House. For a long time Jim stood under the tree, looking down the road where the truck had gone. He shook his head confusedly and turned toward the house. "Dave Crockett's not wantin me not to feed my horse," he muttered.

He went back into the kitchen. He took the lamp and, going into the hall, placed it on the floor beside the sewing table. He got down on his knees as he had seen Ephram do, and touched the claw feet softly. He touched the brass strings of the lyre. He pulled out one of the small drawers. Threads of silk were in it. The colors were bright. He closed the drawer carefully. "A hundred and fifty dollars." The words trailed away.

He went back into the kitchen. From a room adjoining came the impatient nickering of a horse. He entered. In the corner the eyes of five foxes caught the half-light into small red flames. From a shelf near the door he took a few pieces of meat and threw them into the corner. The foxes snatched at the food. The horse nickered insistently and nuzzled his arm. Going back to the kitchen, the boy mixed some bran with warm water and took it into the room. Playfully he held the nose away and then guided it back to the food. He put his face against the mane of the horse.

When he returned to the kitchen he left the door open.

Throwing a piece of wood on the fire, he went to the wig stand and, lifting the hinged top, took out a book. Then he lay down on the hearth, so close to the fire that his hair was a bright blaze with the flames. He opened the book. On the flyleaf was inscribed in large feminine script: 'To James Braxton Boyden, from Harriet Evans.' Softly he rubbed his fingers over the inscription.

Through the opened door of the side room one of the foxes crept, eyes bright and watchful. It crept closer to the boy. It sniffed his shoulder; then curled up close to his arm. The boy turned into the book and began to read:

> At first Robinson Crusoe was afraid to sleep for fear of wild animals. He found a hollow place in the rocky side of a hill, like a shallow cave. He wished he had some skins to cover the opening. He hunted for some logs and carrying them to the cave made a kind of covering. Then he carried all his belongings into the cave. He now felt very safe.

Jim looked up from the book. "A hundred and fifty dollars," he murmured aloud. The fox at his shoulder lifted its head and blinked. "And I might've given it to him, if Dave Crockett had a-said so."

He closed the book with a snap. The fox scurried away toward the door. Rousing himself, he took the lamp and when into the hall. He picked up the little sewing table and mounted the stairs. At the head of the steps he paused before a door. A brass key was in the lock. He turned it and pushed the door open slowly. A few leaves rattled as the door moved back. He stopped. He closed the door and turned the key.

He went down the hall and came to a room cluttered with high beds and chests, and went through this room into another room back of it. He moved a high chest from the wall and, behind it, he placed the little table. Then he opened an old trunk and pulled out an armful of curtains. They smelled of musk. The lace caught on the knob of a chest in passing. Impatiently he jerked it loose. He threw the curtains over the table. Then over these he spread a mass of quilts, and, looking about, moved two smaller chests to the top of the first. Against the door of this room he moved a heavily curtained tester. Anyone not knowing could not tell that there was a door or a room back of the bed.

When he was back in the kitchen, he again sprawled himself before the fire, opened the book and began reading again. While he had been gone, all the foxes had crept into the room. The mother fox once more curled up at his shoulder, the little foxes near the fire, their eyes unblinking and watchful. Absently Jim took the tail of the fox close to his shoulder and brushed its ear. Then he dropped it and turned the pages back to the flyleaf to let his fingers caress the inscription. In a moment, however, he turned back into the book and began reading:

As the days went by poor Robinson felt very sorry for himself. He said: "Here I am all alone. No ship will ever pass this place. Soon I shall even lose count of the days. What shall I do?"

133

So what do you think Robinson did?

He found him a high post and set it up near the shore where he landed. He nailed a board near the top to make it look like a cross.

He knew he had been on the island about ten or twelve days, so with his knife he cut out, "I came on shore . . ."

The winds of March blew high, and in the mountains the Judas trees, red with bloom, glowed in the brown tangle of the limbs of the oaks and maples and pines; swift rains lingered in the glassy needles of the firs and hemlocks and in the bark and rocks and moss along the swollen streams. Folk around the Cove began saying: "Little Squire Jim's comin out of the Valley again. And the way he and that hoss of hissen git through the trees is enough to faze the devil hisself." Til Umbarger reported that he had seen him riding in the night up Cove-end, "a-layin close to the hoss's neck, jest flyin over the gullies, seems like," and Til nodded his head emphatically. "And that's the biggest, wildest hoss I ever seed. Next thing a body knows, he'll be ridin up on Hangin Rock and settin in a streak of lightnin on that hoss till the old Rock falls. Any night now."

Harriet heard these things, and she was troubled. Not since that November afternoon when she had galloped down the road from the Valley had she seen Jim. But embedded in her mind was the memory of him standing motionless, away from the trees of the entrance to the Valley, feet wide apart, hands loosely down, red hair tangled and curling, face flushed and wild; and throughout the days that followed that day, she thought about the moments in the cave. Sometimes she scolded herself. "He was only watching me hold the little fox, wanting to give me something. And now he won't ever come to school again. And I hurt him again." She thought of the strange rudeness of the cave, with its furs and rough stool and luster pitcher, the color 'like your hair,' and of the vixen in the corner of the cave with the four little ones suckling. "He was just lonely and wanted me to see his cave and little foxes," she insisted to herself again, but rising with these thoughts came also the memory of the expression in his eyes, his quickened breathing and the hot closeness of his body. "But even if he had touched me, or put his arms around me, or tried to kiss me even, I could have told him not to." And in the night when she was almost asleep the haunting shadow of his strange, handsome face and the rhythmic movement of his body passed through her dreams.

One day in April the children came in from recess with excited expressions on their faces. "Little Jim's settin on his horse in the woods." Harriet went to the window and looked out. There he was across the road in the trees, motionless on his horse. But in the afternoon he was gone. Several days passed. Then he was there again. Harriet waited longer after school. Perhaps he would come in. But he was gone when she went out. Once, though, she heard soft hoof beats behind her on the road. Far back on the road she saw him. But when he saw her turn, he stopped and swung off into the trees.

That night she went to see Annie Umbarger.

"I've seed him, too," Annie whispered.

"Where did you see him?"

"I seed him not more'n two days ago, lookin behind my hawthorn bush. Aint nobody knows what goes on in that boy's head, but I know what I know this time."

"What is it that you know?" Harriet asked.

Annie's eyes narrowed, and the little glint came into them. "I aint tellin everything I know. But I'm knowin what I know. A pretty girl like you, and it spring, and Little Jim huntin back of my hawthorn bush." She nodded emphatically at Harriet. "Don't never say I aint warned you."

"But what is it you are afraid of? I just want to ask him to come back to school. Tell him I'm sorry I ran away, that—"

Annie nodded her head again, a wise note in her voice. "I've seed wild things grow, right in my yard, an don't never say I aint teched yore ear with a warnin-stick."

And Harriet could get no more from her.

In May she overheard Will Hollister tell Clonda that he had seen Little Jim and his horse under a tree not far from the house, had seen him several times; but when he had called out to him he had received no answer. And once or twice he was sure he had even seen him closer, under the tree across the road from the yard corner. There were scarred hoof marks there, too, clear in the daylight.

Harriet heard these things with beating heart, and at twilight and on into the night she sat in her window listening, watching for some movement in the shadows. But each night Venus, the evening star, large, brilliant and so near the earth, rose over the distant mountain ridge, and Jupiter soon following, and in time the two were lost in flight-and-pursuit in the heavens above the eaves above her window. And still she failed to see Little Jim. "School will be out soon and I'll have to go home," she cried to herself, "and if he doesn't come just once, I'm—" She tried to find some answer. "I'm going down there in the Valley and tell him I'm sorry I ran like that." But the dread of what might be in Little Stepper Valley crept around her in warning words of Annie Umbarger: "Some folks say that pope-preacher never came out of there alive. And I aint sayin it too far around, but I'm thinkin that boy's daddy weren't put in the ground natural, neither, but is still walkin around in that house and ridin the Valley on that black hoss."

The night before the last day of school Harriet sat beside the window. The moon rode clear over the mountain ridge. "And tomorrow's the last day of school," she half-cried, and her fingers ran restlessly over the window sill. Far back in the kitchen part of the house the sounds were scattered and faint. She heard them and yet she did not hear them. Her thoughts were searching down the road. Suddenly, as if out of nothing, she was sure of a mass under a tree a short distance down the road. The light from the moon made ragged shadows along the way, startling her imagination into seeing vaguer forms; with surety she saw a foreleg of a horse, white-socked to the knee, raise itself into a patch of white light under the tree, then strike the turf. With beating heart she made out the shape of the horse and the sheen of bare shoulders and arms against the tree.

Quickly she slipped down the stairs. She sped along the road. As she drew near the tree, she called softly, "Is that you, Jim?" Horse and boy moved out from the tree. He slipped to the ground. In the knowledge of his reality she stopped suddenly, so confused she could only murmur stupidly, "You haven't been to school, Jim. All spring." Then she faltered. "I'm sorry I ran away that day. I don't know what made me."

He came closer, so close she could feel the warmth of his shoulder. She felt suddenly small beside him.

"I've got a thing, just for you," he breathed.

"Something just for me?" Her heart began to beat.

He nodded and motioned toward Little Stepper Mountain. "A yellow thing." There was a shadow of a smile on his face.

"But, Jim, it's dark. I couldn't go," she answered, yet she looked down the road which the moonlight made into a white lane between the trees. "I . . ."

He came closer. "The wood blooms are soft like little ears," he whispered softly, his lips close.

"But . . ."

"And the trillies are white and red inside." His eyes were on her in pleading insistence. "And you can ride the horse . . ."

"You won't hurt me, Jim?" she whispered.

He shook his head.

"Is that a promise?"

He nodded again.

He helped her on the horse, and then, as that other time,

138

he jogged along in front, holding the rein. A short distance into the Valley they left the road and began following the course of the stream. The splashing of the horse in the shallow pools, the click of its shoes on the rocks, were the only sounds. He never once turned to speak, or to look back at her. He seemed determined on some particular place. They came to a deeper pool in the stream. He stopped and removed his trousers to hold them over his head. She was startled to see the whiteness of his back and hips and legs where the sun had not browned them. He waded in. The horse followed. The water touched Harriet's feet. She lifted them to keep them dry. They moved on. The monster trees above were so black that she could hardly see the horse's head, and only the swishing of the water as he moved through it assured her that Jim was there. Soon she heard ahead of them a cascade of falling water. The trees grew open. He led the horse up on the bank. Ahead she could see the cascade which she had only heard a moment before, falling white in the moonlight.

Jim came close to the horse's shoulders. "Get off," he said.

"But, Jim, I'm afraid." Her heart was pounding.

"It's up there." He gestured toward the top of the cascade.

"But Jim . . ."

"It's just up the rocks."

She slid off the horse and, with him close behind, she climbed a rocky ladder that ran up beside the falling water and came suddenly into an opening above. Edged around by heavy trees was a pool of clear water, its farther end shaded by a great shell-like rock. The hemlock and spruce grew thick about it. The bank about it was soft with moss and ferns. She smelled fragrance of wild valley-lilies. The moon, caught for a moment in a sharp cleft between the point of a hemlock and the high edge of the rocky shell, made a silver gleam on the water; and the moss along the bank and leaves and blossoms lay clear in light. She knelt and touched a bloom. The petal was thick as soft fur. She looked into the darker recesses. Trillium, white petals on tall stems, mandrake leaves and wild columbine were tufted close to clumps of pale crested iris, and deep among them, half-hidden, two yellow blooms.

"I fetched them," he said simply.

"Oh," she breathed, "yellow trillium. I never saw a yellow trillium before in all my life. Two of them." And she let her fingers touch them softly.

"And I've got somethin else," he whispered, close to her ear.

"Something else?" and she searched his eyes.

"Not time yet," he breathed.

She let her eyes turn back into the shaded banks. The banks grew darker. The trillium grew shadowy. It seemed that only fragrance lay about the water.

"Now," she finally heard him whisper.

The moon that had been above the shell rock when she came had now waned; a luminous radiance in the sky was all that remained of it. The trees had grown black about the basin.

"In the water," he said.

She dropped her eyes. Deep in the pool the evening star which she had watched nightly climbing over the horizon to lose itself in the heavens above the eaves of her room

140

had now risen over the tips of the hemlocks about the pool and now lay caught in the water. She held her breath in sudden fear that even her breathing would make the water ripple and the star be lost in a myriad fragments.

She turned to look at him, where he sat half-turned from her, partly in shadow, his arms about his knees, the brown of his body merging in the shadows. His face was etched in the light. She tried to pierce the darkness of his eyes, but a sense of their strange, unfathomable depths crept over her and she lay back on the moss, her heart beating with quickened throb. After a time she heard him say, "Take off your things."

Her heart was pounding. Her breathing was uneven. She could only lie quiet, hearing him say the words again and finally adding, "I'll stand over there." She saw him rise and stand with his back to her, deep in the trees. For a long time she lay watching his figure, straight and motionless, until the moments were whirling about her into flashing minutes, and the pounding of her heart seemed beating out eternities. At last she lay back on the moss, white beside the water as the white trillium and the wood violets along its edge.

As in a dream she felt the warmth of his body close to her and, opening her eyes, saw him half-sitting, half-leaning beside her, looking down into her face; but she had no sense of his touching her until fingers burning were on her hair, her cheeks, her throat. Looking up into his face, she smiled and in the fragment of a moment saw in his face an answering smile, momentarily fleeting, no more, so intent were his eyes. She felt him bridging her with his arm. She stirred and touched his arm, and in the touch it seemed the gnarled branches of the forest were weighing him down about her. Fragments of flame leapt up inside her to answer the fire in his eyes. His breath was on her cheeks, on her lips. But in the moment her hand on his arm tensed. Her eyes opened in sudden fright. "Listen," she whispered.

He swung back on his elbows.

Below the cascade came the sound of pawing, rough stamping, and low whinnying. He crept down the rocks.

Trembling, she stood back into the bank. Soon he returned. "Nothin," he said. "My horse standin there, his eyes mean."

"Maybe it was someone hiding." She looked into the trees.

He shook his head.

She was shivering. "I want to go home."

"I tell you it was just my horse standin there."

"But I want to go home."

"It was nothin," he insisted, barring the way.

She looked about her. A thousand tiny stars were in the pool, but the bright star had waned. He still barred the way. "You promised. You promised," she cried.

"I don't want to keep my promise."

"But you said you would. And I'm afraid. I'll come back some time. But it's late, and I'm afraid."

"It was nothin but my horse."

"You promised, Jim," she pleaded. "It's late."

"You'll come back?"

"Yes. I promise. I'll come back."

He went ahead of her down the rock ladder, holding her hand, and when she was on the horse he led her down the stream, retracing their way. On the journey back he did not turn around or speak. At the gate, as she slipped off the horse, she said: "Don't come any nearer. Someone will hear us." She looked up at him. "Do you want to kiss me goodnight?"

He still held the reins. She leaned toward him. Awkwardly, almost shyly, he touched her lips with his. Then swiftly he was on his horse, and she heard the sounds of his galloping down the road.

The house was dark, and she crept up to her room and into bed.

The next morning, however, at breakfast Will Hollister broke a long silence with, "Mighty late fer a school teacher to be comin in after bein out with a boy, and that boy the son of Squire Jim Boyden."

"Now, Will, I told you," Clonda interposed quickly, "hit aint none of yore business."

Harriet made no reply, but that night after supper Will Hollister moved his chair out into the yard and sat there until the shadowy figure on the horse under the tree far down the road was gone.

The next day he loaded Harriet's trunk into a buggy and drove her into Tateboro. When they drew near the Courthouse square in Tateboro she said: "Turn down Hill Street to Ellen Hull's. I'll stay with her until I know." She was crying.

That night the shadow of Jim and horse was again under the tree, and in the nights succeeding. Finally Will saw him ride up to the gate, dismount, and come up to the porch, the horse following him at heel.

"She's been gone a week now, come tomorrow," Will Hollister said, standing on the step.

"She promised."

"I don't know what she promised. But she's gone, and she's not comin back, ef I have my say."

"She promised," Jim repeated, as if Will's words had not been said.

"Go up in her room and look, then," said Will.

Jim did not move for a moment. Then he dropped the rein and, before Will could realize that his words had been taken literally, he heard the boy moving around in her room upstairs.

In a few minutes the sounds in the room ceased. Will backed up against the wall.

In a moment Jim was back down. He leapt on the horse, kicked it in the ribs and, taking the fence in a flying leap, was soon lost down the road.

144

BLOOD STAR

In early June Little Jim rode up to Jonas
Leach's house. It was a log-and-plank house, sharp into the
mountainside, with an apple tree near the porch. Arabel
Leach was on the porch shelling peas. She was barefooted
and her sandy-red hair was plaited over the crown of her
head as she had observed Harriet Evans arrange hers.
When Jim rode up Arabel blushed and lowered her eyes.
She had not seen him since that day in school when he
pulled her hair. Jim rode close to the edge of the porch

and threw an earring into her lap. "I've got another one like it, if you'll come ridin over the hill."

The next afternoon Arabel met him out of sight of the house. She was wearing the single earring. He pulled her up on the horse, holding her in front of him, his arm tight around her.

But when they rode back, near sundown, she sat behind, holding on to him. She wore two earrings; and the next night when she knew his horse was under a tree up the road, she slipped out and met him.

On the side of Sleeping Father Mountain the meadow borders were blue with thistle, and among the rocks wild butterfly was orange to the radiance of a sunset, and horsemint the color of deep magenta. The Totten brothers were pitching hay. Maybelle, just turned fourteen that week, in a broad straw hat was sitting under a tree watching her brothers pitch the hay upon the wagon. At a sound of falling rock and brushing limbs the Tottens looked toward the mountain to see Little Jim on his horse coming precipitously down into the meadow.

"Hi, Little Squire," greeted Broat from the wagonbed.

Jim did not answer the greeting, but only slid off his horse and took the fork from Thag. With swift lift of arm and easy flow of muscle he began pitching the hay up to Broat and Lennert. His shoulders and arms gleamed in the sun. Thag went over to sit under the tree with Maybelle.

"Better'n you were last summer, Little Squire," Thag called. "Shoulders big as yore daddy's. Right proud to know you."

146

Jim pitched on unheeding, with ceaseless rhythm, until the men on top cried: "Stop. Caint git another blade on her to stay."

Jim stopped, and while Broat and Lennert made the last packing on top, Maybelle came up to him with the bucket of water and offered him a dipperful. Her hat had slipped back, and in the sun her light-chestnut hair burned copper. Jim took the dipper, looking over its brim at her. He drank slowly, his eyes on her hair. "Mighty pretty red hair," he said, still holding the dipper at his chin.

"Taint no redder'n yourn," she answered, smiling.

He raised his free hand as if to touch her hair, but Thag interrupted with "Maybelle, you git on the wagon and ride to the house."

Jim watched the wagon go creaking down the meadow. When it was nearly out of sight he said, "My horse wants a drink of water."

"Aint enough in the bucket, Little Squire, fer a hoss."

"Reckon I'll go to the house to get my horse a drink," said Jim, and without further words he mounted and rode down the meadow toward the house.

When the hay wagon came back, Jim did not return with it. "He's under a tree in the backyard givin his hoss a drink of water," said Lennert.

"That tree's gonna fall down and kill him, too, ef he stays there too long," Thag answered darkly. "Were Maybelle in the yard?"

"No," said Broat. "In the house."

In the hot days of July and the cooler nights of August the folk about the Cove began to comment, half-jokingly, half-fearfully. "Little Squire Jim's turnin into a courtin man and lookin more like his daddy every day."

"He aint ridin into Virginny to git a wife, ef he finds what he wants back here," sometimes would be the reply; for at night Jim's horse was pawing under trees near a great many houses in and around the Cove. Mothers began to watch their daughters with wary eyes. If by chance Jim rode by in the daytime, and if one of the girls moved to the porch to see him, her mother was certain to point out, "Now, you've not got red hair on yore head."

"Don't have to have red hair to git Little Squire Jim to notice. Jest got to have a streak of it. Look at Arabel Leach and Sudie Holt."

But their fathers were more direct. "Ef I ketch one of you girls standin under a tree talkin to Big Squire's son, I'll beat the livin stuffin out of you."

But threats or warnings or not, if in the night one of the girls saw Jim and his horse under a tree, or heard a low whistle like the call of a lonely bird, she would slip out into the dark.

In the middle of September Will Hollister mentioned to his wife, "Seem like I seed Little Jim and his hoss under the tree down our road agin last night."

"Whyn't you look fer hoof marks?"

"I did, and the ground's all tore up with pawin."

"Next time you see him, ask him what he's waitin fer," Clonda said.

"I reckon I already know without askin."

"Don't do no harm to ask. I feel kinda sorry fer him."

The next night when Will was sure he saw the shadow

148

under the tree, he walked down the road and climbed the bank. Little Jim sat motionless on his horse.

"Anything I ken do to favor you, Little Squire?" Will asked.

"No."

"Ef I could, it'd pleasure me."

The boy did not answer. Will did not know whether to persist or to return to the house without saying anything more. Finally he said hesitantly, "Ef you're waitin fer that school teacher, Little Squire, I ken tell you she aint comin back."

Some subtle movement of the boy's body made the horse jerk a step forward suddenly, but Jim pulled the rein, stopping it short.

"Jest thought I'd tell you," said Will.

"This your road?"

"Why, Little Squire, I aint meanin anything like that," Will answered, hurt. "Ride yore hoss in my yard. Come set awhile with me and Clonda. Eat awhile. Welcome anytime. I was jest sayin that school teacher's not comin back, that's all."

Boy and horse remained motionless.

Will backed awkwardly down the bank and went to his house.

The next night he saw boy and horse under the tree, and on successive nights, until school opened. But Will did not go down the road to disturb him again. "Ef he aint wantin to take my word for it, he ken find out for hisself," said he to his wife.

On the morning the school on the hill was to open, the earliest child arriving found Little Jim astride his horse beside the iron bell in the yard. He wore his father's gray-and-yellow shirt. His hair seemed to have been troubled. The children spoke to him, for during the summer Jim's friendliness in the Cove made them feel safer with him. But Jim was stonily unresponsive to their greeting, and they fell back. The old uneasiness crept over them. When others arrived, they whispered to each other and avoided with their eyes the horse and rider beside the bell. At last the new teacher came, a tall, sharp-featured, elderly woman, with an aggressive stride. She unlocked the door. She spoke to one of the boys, Jody Campbell, and, nodding toward the bell, strode inside. Jody came toward Little Jim. When he was within a few yards he heard Jim say, "You're not touchin this bell."

Jody faltered. He was not prepared for the tone. After all, his sister Lilymae had giggled every time Jim's name was mentioned during the summer, and she was wearing a bracelet and a finger-ring. But he backed away. The other children were already crowding into the school. In a few minutes Little Jim remained alone in the yard. An hour passed. Then he urged the horse forward. At the school steps he slipped off, and, holding the rein in his hand, went just inside the doorway. Miss Arkwright looked up from her desk.

"Young man," she said, "if you've come to school, come in and sit down."

He searched the room. His gaze returned to the desk where Miss Arkwright was sitting. Then swiftly, so swiftly there was hardly time to wink an eye, he was on his horse, and those in the room saw through the door a rearing arc of boy and horse, red hair and checked shirt and bay haunches a fused whirl; heard sharp thuds of hoofs on the turf and wild galloping ringing out down the road.

"Shut the door," Miss Arkwright said to the boy nearest the back.

After that Will Hollister did not see Jim and his horse near his house, nor did he see any fresh hoof marks. October turned into November and not only Will but no one else in or around the Cove caught even a glimpse of him or his horse. But it was whispered about that Eldo was seen outside a cabin up Crivet Creek way. No one knew much about those who lived in the cabin, for it had been empty a long time, except that the man's name was Beldie Thomas, that he was married, and that his wife had red hair and was pretty.

However, difficulties began to be apparent nearer home. One dark night in the second week of November the Totten brothers rode through the rocks into Little Stepper Valley. They rode close together. They carried their guns. Their talking was sparse. They rode around to the back and dismounted. Thag called out, "Little Squire, we've come to talk to you about somethin."

The door opened and Little Jim stood in the doorway. The dying coals from the fire inside gave a soft reddish glow in back of him. There was something of the Big Squire in the way he stood in the door frame, silent and motionless, his head and shoulders seeming enormous in the shadows.

The Totten men huddled close together. Finally Thag said: "Hit's about Maybelle. She's in trouble, and we've come to ask you what you aimed to do about it."

The figure in the doorway gave no other answer than to lean one shoulder against the frame. Thag handed his pistol to Broat. "I'm goin close and talk to him." He went forward to the kitchen door, and Lennert and Broat heard him talking in a low voice to the boy. Then he turned angrily and came back across the yard to his brothers. "He says he's not old enough to git married."

"He's old enough to git a girl in trouble," Lennert said.

"And he's as old as me, and I'm sixteen," Broat threw in.

They were interrupted with Little Jim's calling from the door. "Go ahead and shoot. I'm not afraid of bein killed."

Thag broke away from his brothers. Anger was in his voice, and he moved toward Jim threateningly. "I'm aimed to do hit, by God. But first, I'll give you a chance to make out yore will, and let you git on yore knees in front of that there idol you got in there in the corner."

"Land and stuff to the Catholic Church and Old Lady Gwynn if I'm killed before I'm grown," Jim answered without moving.

"That the way yore ma fixed her will?" Thag asked.

When Jim did not answer, Thag turned uncertainly toward his brothers. Thag was a Foot-washing Baptist and in his mind the Pope and the Devil were two of a piece. The whole Catholic structure to him was a sinister force, an invisible swamp mist, creeping into honest people's hearts and homes, leading them to eternal damnation.

"I'm not settin out to help the Catholic Church," Thag shouted. His brothers moved closer toward him. "But let me tell you somethin, Jim Boyden," he angrily went on.

152

"You think jest cause you're the Big Squire's son, and ownin a whole slice of the county, you're better'n folks around here that's honest and hard-workin. Settin yoreself up higher'n God Almighty. Runnin wild like a animal. Ridin over folks' places, and gitten their girls in trouble. But to me you aint nothin atall. Nothin atall. Not even good as a hound dog wallerin in a ditch. When a man's got everything in the world cept sense—and I reckon you aint got a drop of that, got everything in the world cept sense—and then gits a girl in trouble and jest stands in the door and says, 'Go ahead and shoot,' he aint fitten to be killed. Not fitten to be killed."

Jim stirred in the doorway as if something of Thag's angry words had penetrated. He took a step outside the doorway. The Totten men drew closer.

"Not right, little Maybelle not havin a man around her house, if she's in trouble," he muttered.

The Totten men remained silent, waiting.

"And Ludy Shelton's a hard-workin man," he went on.

"But Ludy's never set in my house once," Thag interrupted. "And what's more—"

"You ever see me in your house?" Jim asked quickly.

"No, but—"

"And he's old enough to get married."

"But—"

Jim shifted in the doorway. "And he's not doin right not marryin," he continued, rubbing his hand through his hair. "And he's not doin right not marryin Maybelle, and her sweet and in trouble— Give me that gun."

And before Lennert realized what he was doing Jim

153

stepped out of the door, came close, and took the shotgun from his hands and was inside the house and slamming the door, leaving them looking at each other.

"First time I ever heared him talk so much in all my born days," Thag said stupidly, and before the Totten men could comprehend the swift direction of Jim's reasoning, they heard Eldo pounding around the corner of the house with Jim on his back.

A half-hour later Ludy Shelton was startled to hear a voice shouting in the yard outside. "Come on out under a tree and talk some." Ludy did not recognize the voice, nor did he like the tone of the words. He lay still in his bed. "You want me to ride in and fetch you out?" the voice called.

In time Ludy came to the door, but even under a tree he was sullen.

"But I aint been keepin company with Maybelle Totten. Never once."

"And you're old enough to get married," Jim argued.

"But I'm tellin you—"

"I'm all worn out with arguin," Jim broke in. "You're not doin right by little Maybelle. I'll give you a bed and some dishes to set up with, and if it's a boy I'll give you a piece of land if I'm not killed before I can keep it away from Old Lady Gwynn."

Ludy became thoughtful, and when the Tottens rode up he pretended to be surprised to see them in his yard in the middle of the night, but since they were there, he would like to speak a word or two to them about marrying their sister. After some parley, when the Tottens

154

were ready to leave, Thag asked, "Seen anything of Little Jim in a month or two?"

"Taint fer me to answer to the Little Squire's comins and goins," Ludy answered. "May be settin on Old Hangin Rock this minute."

"Lennie's gun's here, leanin against a tree," Broat interrupted.

"Lennie must've fetched it when he come," said Ludy. "Fox huntin?"

"No," said Lennert. "Jest ridin fer the night air."

Three days later Ludy and Maybelle were married, and the day after the wedding a sledge with Eldo dragging it and Jim leading the horse pulled up in front of Ludy's house. The sledge was full. Jim and Ludy carried in a heavy walnut bed with ornately carved pineapples on the four posts. "I brought some rope and bed things," Jim said, "and this chest here with glass knobs. And some silver things to set around. And some dishes."

Ludy beamed with pleasure, but Maybelle burst out angrily: "I'm not knowin why you fetch yore old stuff over here to my house, Jim Boyden. And I'm sayin ef I want a curtain over my bed or not, or pineapples on the posts. But, Jim Boyden, I'm not wantin dishes with writin on em, and I don't want them cups what's not got handles on em."

"But the cups shine in the light like—" and he looked at her dull-copper braids.

"I aint carin about shine. And I don't want that dish with the feathers and pope-writin on it."

155

Jim put the cups back into the crested bowl and, holding them under his arm, stood looking at her for a moment. Then abruptly he turned and went outside.

"An don't come round here with no more cups without flowers," Maybelle called after him.

However, the next day when he brought the cups with handles and flowers, he found Maybelle alone. She was quiet, and said simply: "Jim, I aint mad with you, but I aint wantin Ludy to be thinkin I want you to be bringin me things. I aint carin ef cups have handles or no. I'm not mad, Jim."

Jim shifted from one foot to the other. Finally he said, "Maybelle, I never meant to get you in trouble."

"I know you aint, Jim. And I'm much obliged."

"And if it's a boy, I'll give him some land soon's I'm old enough."

"I'm much obliged, Jim."

He moved out on the step. "Take care of yourself, Maybelle." Then he swung on his horse and galloped off.

But in December when Sims Holt and his two sons, and later Lew Campbell and his brother rode into the Valley and knocked on the door of Little Stepper House, there was no answer. They walked angrily around the house, pounding the front door, trying the downstairs windows, but they could get no response. They eyed the open windows of the upstairs room. They shouted, "Ef you're up there in that room asleep, come on down here and talk to honest folks what's troubled." There was no answer.

There was nothing to do but to ride back home. But the morning after Wilda Holt was married to Lawson

156

Moore, Sims Holt found in his yard, under a tree close to his house, a tester-bed, a chest of drawers, two chairs, a pile of dishes, three bone-handled knives and forks, and a few spoons; and when Susan Campbell was married, the same number of pieces lay piled near the house the morning after the marriage.

But when Arabel Leach was married the guests sat up all night waiting for Little Jim to bring his wedding gift. They kept careful watch, and the next morning when the sun came up there was nothing.

"Reckon the Little Squire's run out of beds," a half-sober friend of Zeb Faison, the groom, remarked. "Maybe yore first one's gonna have yeller hair like yore own."

Zeb scowled. "You better look to yore own doorstep."

However, a week later, when the sun came up, outside Zeb Faison's cabin were the tester-bed, chest of drawers, chairs, dishes, knives and forks as for the others; and to these were added a pie-crust table, a third chair, and a silver caster with crystal jars.

January, February. And in the early days of March Til Umbarger climbed up to the very edge of Hanging Rock to gather trailing arbutus for his wife. And later, in April, Annie herself went into the mountain crevices to find blue-eyed grass to plant among her wild iris and dog-toothed violets. And in the warm days of May she sang and mumbled among her vines and flowers, glancing over her shoulder brightly, straightening up quickly to look behind her, hoping to find a shadow along the grass or on her gray split-rail fence. But Little Jim never came to sit under her lilac bush or to sprawl along the fence. "Seem like Little Jim'd come and set in my flowers jest one day, fore he gits killed, jest to pester me a mite," she wailed to her husband. But Til only looked toward Little Stepper Valley and shook his head sadly, for seldom a week passed that someone didn't tell of seeing Jim's stallion standing outside Beldie Thomas' plank-and-log house far up the mountain toward Crivet Creek way, daytime or nighttime.

If Beldie Thomas knew during the winter months and the spring months that were passing that Little Jim was coming to his house while he was over in Virginia saw-milling, he never let it be known to Hesterlee. Every other week he came home on Friday with his pay, stayed from Saturday to Sunday, and whatever may have been his thought about the increasing furnishings in the house—a set of bone-handled knives and forks, china, an occasional chair—his interest was casual. "Jest some old junk folks are givin me," Hesterlee explained. "Don't do no harm to take what folks don't want."

That May, however, when Annie Umbarger was singing her songs of wistful hope in her garden, Hesterlee saw Beldie Thomas one morning examining carefully the ground in the yard near the porch. "Looks like a hoss been pawin around my house," he observed.

"Jest some folks comin to see me now and then," Hesterlee answered. "You're not wantin me to set here all day long and night time too seein nobody, would you?"

"Whyn't you come on over where I work and live? I aint afeared no more."

158

"I like it here," she answered. She was pretty, with hair soft and glowing to a faint red, and she was slow in movement and liked to stay in one place, if she could.

In late June, when the twilight was a purple mist in the trees, Beldie came home a day early, on a Thursday, to find her dressed in her best dress, and wearing eardrops and a bracelet. Her hair was brushed to a glow. "Jest some stuff I had fore I come off up here with you," she explained.

He looked at her with half-closed eyes. "Some things I heared since I been around here git put together all at once," he said.

Under his gaze she grew uneasy. "I aint knowin what you be talkin about," she answered. But after supper she slipped off through the woods and came onto the road, a quarter of a mile toward Little Stepper Mountain. Two small logs stood against a birch tree whose bark gleamed white even in the night. She pushed the two logs so that they fell across the ditch and extended to the edge of the road. Then she hurried back along a path that cut through to the house. A short distance in she reached down and released a branch of a tree which had been caught back with a thong. The branch sprang across the path. Anyone walking or riding along the path would strike it full in passing. Then through the trees she made a wide curve and came in back of the house. By the lamp Beldie was busy with his gun. In the faint light his sharp nose and receding chin suggested some sharp-nosed animal, brown and wily. He did not look up, but kept his eyes on the gun.

"Seem like it took you a long time to go out back," he said.

159

"I'm not beholden to you fer where I go every minute," she answered.

He tried the mechanism of the gun. The hammer snapped sharply.

"I'm goin to bed," she said.

He put the gun in the corner. "Reckon I will too, then."

On the following Sunday afternoon Beldie made no preparation to leave.

"Aint you goin back over the mountain to work?" she asked.

"Not lessen you go with me," he answered.

"I'm not plannin to leave this place yet awhile," she answered.

"I reckon I aint neither, then," he replied.

And through late June and into the weeks of July the warning logs lay across the ditch into the road, and Little Squire Jim sat on the steps of Little Stepper House watching the sun sink red and yellow above the mountains. The night was cool. He moved his legs restlessly. A bird called from the far trees. Out of the hollows, along the foothills, shadows began creeping toward the more open spaces about his house. The red-and-yellow splendor faded into a rose, then into a luminous indigo suffused with purple. Over the far crest of Big Stepper Mountain that nosed so close to Hanging Rock a heavy star glowed red, like a fever. Jim stood up. Abruptly he went inside the kitchen room, looked at the empty dishes and utensils, at the flickering candle under the crucifix. Then he went outside again to sit on the doorstep. He stretched one leg out and leaned against the doorframe. Back of the trees and roof of the old slave cabins the moon rose, and soon its light fell across his shoulder and arms. A whippoorwill called in the woods. He watched the red star over Hanging Rock. It was sinking rapidly.

Suddenly he stood up. He went to the back room and slipped the bridle on Eldo. He sprang on the horse's back and, kicking his heels into its sides, urged it forward. Down the road, across an open field, through tree-bordered ways they raced, toward the red star over Hanging Rock. Little Jim lay close against Eldo's neck. Branches tore at his back and shoulders. The stallion's mane whipped itself in stinging stripes across his face and tangled itself in his hair.

Across the Cove road they pounded, breaking the moon path on Blue Snake River into a myriad of diamonded fragments. Up the sides of Sleeping Father Mountain. When the stallion came upon the crest of the mountain, it began following a path through the shrubs. It galloped on, breathing hard. The broad fissure between the mountain cliff and Hanging Rock loomed up before them. Behind them. The stallion came to a sudden stop on Hanging Rock.

The moon, high over the Cove, fell on the flatness of the Rock and struck the boy and horse into silver.

He dropped the rein and walked swiftly to the edge. Blackness fell off the Rock's edge. Far below, Blue Snake River was only a thin, broken wire of silver, threading the trees in the moonlight. Along the Cove road a few yellow eyes of lamplight blinked. But far to the left, where he knew Beldie Thomas' house stood, the mountain was black. Jim looked long toward it, trying to discern a flicker of light that would tell him something. Only darkness was

161

there, and at his feet enormous blackness welling up out of the Cove below the cliff of the Rock.

He turned and came back to the horse. His hand moved over its nose and forehead. He removed his trousers and with them began rubbing the flakes of foam from its chest and back and haunches, until the coat was smooth silver in the night. He let the wet clothing fall to the Rock and he walked back on the edge of the Rock. Out of the Valley a soft breeze moved about his naked hips and ribs, the pits of his arms. He leaned farther over the edge, far over. His horse shifted its haunches and whinnied. Drawn back, the boy returned to the horse. He threw the bridle over its head, and mounting, backed it to the front edge of the Rock.

At the signal the horse sprang forward, its hoofs rattling the table of rock in short bucking steps to gain speed, to make a mighty leap across the fissure, to land on the cliff-side, to lose itself in the brush and trees down the mountainside.

When they came back into Little Stepper Valley Eldo was spent. Jim slid off and led the horse to its stall, smoothing its coat again, throwing over it a loose blanket. As he came around to his door again he paused to glance toward the mountain where he knew Beldie Thomas' house was, dark behind its trees. He entered the kitchen. The candle under the crucifix flickered. "I'm goin to get killed sometime," he muttered aloud.

He went to a chest and, hunting under some heavy clothes, found a pistol. He laid it on the table. Then he took a pair of trousers from a hook, and when he had belted them on, he paused. He put on a shirt, and then a pair of shoes. He lighted a candle and held it before a mir-ror to see his shirt buttoned to the neck. "Not goin to be killed naked," he muttered again. He blew out the candle, picked up the pistol and went out the door. The horse moved heavily at seeing him again, but pushed its nose up close. Jim slipped on the bridle, and leading it out, swung on its back.

Near Beldie Thomas' house he saw the logs still lying across the ditch, as if carelessly fallen. He got off and kicked one into the ditch. Then he pushed on. At the path near the house he turned off through the trees. A limb struck the horse and brushed him heavily in the face. He pushed it aside impatiently and urged Eldo on. When he came to the opening before the cabin, he pulled up under an oak and called out, "I've come to make a visit."

He could hear no movement in the house. Then he called out again, "I've come to make a visit."

A stumbling over a chair inside, and a short delay. Then Beldie appeared in the door, half-dressed.

"What you want this time of night?"

"I've come to talk a spell with Hesterlee."

Beldie put his hand on the door edge. "We've gone to bed and we don't want no company." The door closed.

Jim pushed his horse up the steps until its front feet clattered on the porch. "You want me to tie my horse to a tree out here, or ride through the front door?" The horse's hoofs shook the porch boards.

From inside came Hesterlee's voice. "Leave the horse under a tree. Not room in here. Too many folks around here now." A slow light of a lamp flickered.

Jim backed his horse down, and dropped the reins over

its head. He went up on the porch, pushed the door open. Beldie stood back of the opening.

"Hesterlee wants me to come in," said Jim.

Beldie moved surlily over. Jim looked around the dimly lit room. Hesterlee was standing near the mantel holding the lamp. Her red hair fell in a loose red-gold cascade over her shoulders, and her eyes, deerlike and dark, were wide in fear. She was breathing rapidly, and as she moved a step nearer the mantel Jim sensed the flowering of her body under her thin gown. He stood in the middle of the room looking at her. He seemed impervious to Beldie back of him. A look of panic flared in Hesterlee's eyes, and she made an impulsive gesture. Jim turned quickly. Beldie was moving to a corner of the room, toward his gun. Jim stepped in front of him.

Checked, Beldie demanded angrily, "Who do you think you are, come bustin into a man's house this time of night?"

"Why're you stayin home so long?"

"A man's got a right to stay home in his own house, aint he?"

Jim for a moment did not answer. Hesterlee put the lamp on the mantel. She glanced from Beldie to Jim. "He's nothin but a boy," she said softly to Beldie. "Don't you see?"

Beldie swept Jim with his eyes. Taken unaware for a moment by Hesterlee's words, Jim rubbed his hand through his hair and moved uncertainly. His face seemed confused; then it darkened somberly. For a moment it seemed he would disappear from the room. Then he picked up a chair and slid it across the floor into the corner in front of the gun. Taking another chair, he reversed it, and sat down between Beldie and the corner, his arms on the back of the chair.

Hesterlee moved a little toward Beldie, her voice persuasive. "Go out in the yard, Beldie, a minute. Jest a minute."

"I want to talk to Hesterlee some," Jim added quickly. "But I'm not aimin to be killed by a shot gun. I brought you a pistol to do the shootin with." He pulled the pistol from his belt. "I'd a-brought you somethin else, but I got to thinkin about Hesterlee and come right off without doin it."

Beldie leaned against the door. He shook his head slightly as if he didn't understand the words. "You mean you aimin to let me shoot you with yore own gun?"

Jim turned the chair around and sat in it again. He crossed his leg and took off a shoe, and let it fall to the floor. "G'on out in the road. I want to talk to Hesterlee." He let the other shoe fall. He kept his eyes on Beldie. Suddenly he raised his voice in anger. "You're not actin like any man I ever heard of. You can keep the pistol even." He put both feet on the floor and looked steadily at Beldie.

Beldie flared. "You're the damnedest, low-downdest fool I ever come acrost. An damned ef I don't kill you, ef it's the last thing I do."

"I'm goin to talk to Hesterlee first." Jim's voice was soft.

There was a pause. Finally Beldie asked, "How long you want, fore I kill you?"

"How long you reckon?" asked Jim.

Hesterlee interrupted. "Go on out in the road and smoke a cigarette, Beldie."

"Smoke two or three," Jim said quickly.

"I aint got but one," Beldie objected.

165

From the mantel Hesterlee took an opened package. She handed the cigarette to Jim. "Not but five left," she said.

"And you've got one," Jim said to Beldie. He put the cigarettes in the chair seat and stood back.

But Beldie did not move. "I'm not gonna take but two."

"Take em all."

"I aint gonna do it."

"Five."

"Two."

"Take em all. What's four left when you're aimin to kill a man?" There was a faint suggestion of a smile in his eyes.

"Reckon so," Beldie agreed, his tone almost friendly as he picked them up. Suddenly he flared up again. "But gimme that pistol."

"I'm keepin the pistol till you get across the road," Jim answered. "And soon as you light up I'll put it on the step out there. And soon as you get through smokin, come on over and shoot."

Beldie backed out the door, blinking his eyes.

"I'm not good at countin," said Jim, "but I can count to six."

Beldie backed into the yard. Jim followed him to the door.

When Beldie had settled himself under a tree across the road, the cigarette tip glowing, Jim placed the pistol on the lower front step, and came back up into the room.

"Jim," Hesterlee said plaintively, "I never meant that about you bein jest a boy. You're not a boy to me."

Jim did not answer for a moment but continued standing where he could see the cigarette glow under the tree.

166

Finally he said, "I'm old enough." Then he added, his voice caressing, "Put out the light, Hesterlee, and come over here close."

She blew out the flame, and when she came near him he put his arm around her waist and kissed her; and then drawing her closer and tighter, he lifted her in his arms.

"Jim, we mustn't," she cried. "I'll get him away tomorrow, and you ken come back." He only held her tighter.

"Come over here on the edge of the bed, so I can look out the door, and I'll tell you somethin, the kind of things you like to hear about the stars and wild honey, and soft green water, and lightnin, and ridin in the night in the silver trees—"

"But Jim—"

He lifted her up and carried her to the bed. "He's just smokin the first one, and I'm sure goin to tell you about red and yellow clouds holdin up the sky when it's green and yellow, and the sun settin on the mountain and not carin about a thing but the clouds turnin on fire . . ."

Across the road, under a pine tree, Beldie Thomas lit his second cigarette with the stub from the first. "He's the damnedest fool I ever run acrost in all my born days," he thought. "Not even got good sense. Acts like nothin I ever run acrost or seed. Jest aint a natural man." He stirred and muttered aloud. "But I'm aimin to kill him ef it's the last thing I do fore I die. I'm aimin to do it," and the muttered words were broken only by the nervous puffs on the cigarette.

At the end of the second, and on the lighting of the third, he shifted his back against the tree. Thoughts of a half-lighted room in Tennessee, drinking, sudden blaze of anger and a knife, driving through rain in a buggy, and Hesterlee sniveling by his side, wrapped in a quilt to keep off the rain. The train in the night, and Hesterlee still crying. Beldie shook the ashes sharply from the cigarette. "He were a pizen mean man," he muttered, "and not fitten to live. And I'd do hit agin. And cut his innards out, ef I'd had time. But they didn't ketch me. Aint ketchin me now, lessen . . . I oughtn't to set out and git in trouble over here," he said aloud, suddenly. "And git the law after me agin, sendin me back over there, maybe, ef they don't git me in the chair. Taint worth it. He aint got no sense. He don't act like a man. And he don't look like a man neither." The thought of the horse's clatter on his porch, and the voice calling out flashed through his mind again, and a sharp flush of anger speared up. "Ridin up in my house and talkin to me like that. By God, I'm aimed to kill him, ef—" but the flush of anger died out at the thought of quick flight through the hills. "Taint worth it. And I don't know where else I could git to." He leaned harder against the tree and called out, "Four down, and two to go."

"But I'll make him gimme that pistol, and me and Hesterlee ken clear out at break of day. And somebody else ken kill him ef they want, and git the law after em. I aint aimed to. Besides, he don't act like any natural man I ever knowed. Don't even look growed up, cept in a way about the face."

Almost an hour had passed. He puffed the last cigarette slowly. He stood up. "But I'm aimin to make him gimme that pistol jest the same." In the road he called, "I'm comin acrost."

He moved up the path. He heard no sound within. The pistol lay on the bottom step. He picked it up, and holding it to his side, called again. "I'm comin in, and I want to do some talkin."

He heard feet on the floor, the scrape of a chair, and Jim called out: "Come on in and shoot. I don't feel like talkin. I'm gonna put up a fight, and you shoot."

"I don't want no fight," Beldie answered. He was standing in the door.

"But I'm not goin to get killed without puttin up a fight."

Beldie stepped in. He held the pistol a little to the front of him. In the faint light of the window and door he could see Hesterlee crouched on the bed, the quilt pulled across her breast. In the center of the room a great shadow loomed, moved toward him, and Beldie felt himself caught on the shoulder and waist. "Shoot before I throw you out the door."

Beldie felt his arms caught against Jim's body, the pistol between them. Anger flared up. He tried to draw his arms free, and in doing so he pulled the trigger.

Hesterlee screamed and climbed off the bed. She ran to the window. "Get a light," she heard. She began crying hysterically, but she managed to scratch a match to light the lamp. In the center of the room both men stood, clutched together, but as Jim loosened his arms Beldie slipped to the floor. Across Jim's waist was a black powder burn and blood. But on the floor Beldie lay twitching, a

169

bleeding hole below the heart. Jim looked stupidly down at the body at his feet.

"I never meant to hurt Beldie," he said vacantly.

But Hesterlee cried at him. "Git out. Git out of here. Git out of my house. You've got me in trouble agin. I don't want you around here." She pushed him toward the door. "Git out. Git out," she screamed.

Confusedly he jumped on his horse and rode down the path. At the road he turned and called back. "I never meant to hurt him, I tell you." But as there was no answer, he jogged down the road. "I never meant to hurt him."

Two days later Sheriff Taylor and four men rode into the Valley. Dave Crockett was with them. They left the four men down the road, out of sight of Little Stepper House, and only Sheriff Taylor and Dave went up to the kitchen door. Sheriff Taylor knocked. Little Jim opened the door.

"Little Jim," said Sheriff Taylor, "I knew your daddy, and my daddy knew your grandaddy, and I hate to do it, but I've got a warrant for you. I want you to go along with me."

Jim's eyes were dark and somber.

"We jest come along to see that you don't do anything you're not wantin to do," said Dave.

Jim turned his eyes toward Sheriff Taylor. "I never meant to hurt Beldie," he said.

"I know," Sheriff Taylor replied calmly; "but it's right for you to go along and tell that to the folks that have the say."

Jim's glance swung toward Dave, then back to Sheriff Taylor. "Reckon I'll put on a shirt," he said abruptly.

They heard him moving around inside. Then he came out. He was wearing a gray-and-yellow checked shirt. Dave recognized it as one he had seen on the Big Squire many times.

"I'll take care of things, Little Squire," Dave said. He looked up at the windows on the second floor. "You didn't shet them winders up there. You might be gone more'n a day or two, and hit might rain."

Jim stopped short. "I'm not goin if anybody's goin to meddle in my house."

"I weren't aimin to tech anything you don't want me to," Dave answered quickly. "Ef you want, nobody'll go in yore house."

"That a promise, Dave Crockett?"

"Ef I die to keep it."

"Then I'll be proud to be beholden to you."

"Hit's a favor to me, Little Squire."

"Just take care of my horse till I get back."

Dave nodded.

Dave watched him go down the road with Sheriff Taylor. When they had disappeared Dave looked toward Hanging Rock jutting against the sky in the distance, clear and heavy in the bright sun.

"Ef Old Hangin Rock had-a jest fell on me first," he muttered.

HANGING ROCK
TREMBLES

It didn't take the news of Beldie Thomas' death long to spread through the mountains. According to Ollie Montgomerie, Hesterlee Thomas had pounded on his door in the middle of the night, crying for help and saying Little Squire Jim had killed Beldie. The Cove folk heard Ollie's account in consternation. They had worried about Little Jim's horse standing outside Beldie Thomas' house. They had even intimated in their words that Little

Jim would come to some grief in this adventure with Beldie's redheaded wife. Hadn't his father, the Big Squire, been killed by some woman's husband on the outskirts of Tateboro and hadn't her hair been red, too? But no Boyden had ever been killed the same way twice. There had been comfort in that thought. Little Jim would live his time. Then he would be killed. There was no telling what he might take it into his head to do at his funeral even; but being implicated in a murder and accused of killing a man had never been in the pattern of their thought. Boydens didn't kill. They got killed.

Nevertheless Beldie Thomas was dead, and lying on a plank in that house on Crivet Creek. And his blood was there on the floor, and where the blood had run into the cracks it was still moist. Any way a man looked—on the floor, on the laying-out plank—Beldie Thomas was a dead man and that was as certain as Old Hanging Rock scowling high above Dave Crockett's grist-mill. And Jim's pistol was there in the room along with a gray-and-yellow checked shirt. They looked up to see if Old Hanging Rock was trembling also. But Little Jim didn't wear a shirt in the summertime, or shoes. Hanging Rock steadied itself.

Til Umbarger would not accept the story Hesterlee told. "The Little Squire were not there at the time she says," he cried passionately, his narrow face pale, his hands making futile gestures of denial. "He were flyin the mountains. I saw him on Old Hangin Rock, no tellin how long at the time she says. The dawg-star were jest goin behind the mountain."

"What were you doin out on the mountain that time of night?" Ollie Montgomerie wanted to know.

"I'm not a-tellin everything I know," Til cried, "but I were on Sleepin Father Mountain at the time that woman says Beldie were killed. And I heared a breakin of bushes, and a poundin of hoss's feet. Then there were the Little Squire passin me, ridin fer the cliff. 'He's gonna fall off and never know,' stuck in my mind, and before I knew what I were doin, I were climbin and scratchin after him. And when I got to the edge of the cliff, there he were, the Little Squire and his hoss, settin out on Old Hangin Rock."

"Jumped the cliff to the Rock?" Ollie gasped. "And it wider than a man could stretch with a twenty-foot log?"

Til nodded.

"Did the Rock start teeterin?" Martha Crockett asked, her face pale.

"Hit did not," Til asserted.

"What did you see next?" Ollie persisted.

"The two of em out there on that Rock, clear as two day things in the night. Then the Little Squire walked to the edge of the cliff, not afeared or nothin. And then he come back and took off his britches and rubbed the sweat off the hoss's back and sides till hit were one shine in the moon. The two of em were one silver-shine on the Rock."

To prove his words, Til took Ollie Montgomerie and Dave Crockett with him to the top of Sleeping Father Mountain, to the very cliff edge, pointing to the mound of clothing lying clear in the sunlight.

"I tell you, he weren't at that woman's house. He were a-flyin the mountains on that wild hoss of hissen. Aint that proof of my words, out there on that Rock? How do you know, or anybody know, that that red-headed woman aint makin up words to suit herself?"

"But Beldie Thomas is a-layin out on a plank. And the law's come and took the Little Squire to town," Ollie repeated.

"How's the law gonna tech the Little Squire, lessen it suits him?" Til argued.

"But the law took him."

"The Little Squire ken change his mind, caint he? Did you ever see a man that knowed how Little Squire's mind was gonna work?"

Ollie Montgomerie and Dave Crockett were silent. There was no answer to that.

However, when Dave Crockett walked back to his mill the words of Til Umbarger, 'no law ken tech Little Squire Jim,' kept going through his mind. He looked up toward Hanging Rock, hovering so ominously high above his mill. A cloud was drifting by its brow. "Sometime hit's gonna fall," Dave muttered, "ef I don't watch out."

He crossed the road to his house. "I'm goin to town to see how the Little Squire is farin," he said to his wife.

"Whyn't you take Thag Totten along with you?" she asked.

Dave looked at her in surprise.

"Aint Thag Totten Little Squire's kin folks, one way you look at it?" Martha said.

"Thag never mentioned it to me," Dave evaded.

"Hit always takes two to git in the kind of trouble May-belle was in," Martha said. "And Thag Totten's never been a man not to stand by his kin folks."

"I'll speak to him," Dave answered.

When he came back that night he nodded to Martha. "Thag's gonna do his part."

The next morning, although Dave was up earlier than usual, Thag Totten was already waiting for him at the mill porch. Martha followed Dave to the road. She held out a package. "I cooked the Little Squire some sweet cakes, jest in passin," she said.

"I might be a day or two," Dave answered.

"Take a week ef it comes to it," she said. "A week or two. Howdy, Thag."

"Howdy, Martha Crockett."

"You men folks look to the Little Squire. He's not used to town ways."

In Tateboro Thag and Dave hitched their horses at the side of the Courthouse.

Dave pointed to the window with the lettering *Richard E. Todd, Attorney-at-law* in a gold semi-circle across the glass. They climbed the stairs.

"Lawyer Todd's busy," a girl at the desk said without looking up.

"We'll wait," said Dave. "A week or two."

In a little while the door opened and Richard Todd came out. He was a large man, square about the shoulders. In a general way he was a handsome man, too, with wavy hair beginning to gray above the ears, and eyes behind his glasses keen and swift.

"Do you wish to see me?" he asked, standing aside, inviting them by his glance into his office.

Dave and Thag went ahead of him. "We've come to talk about Little Squire Jim," said Dave.

"Mrs. Gwynn's nephew?"

Dave nodded. "He's her kin, but we're not countin on

that." He hesitated. "Ef Little Squire were back up to the Cove, he could take keer of himself, but—" and Dave hesitated again. "Maybe the Little Squire don't know the way of town laws."

"I've come to stand bail for him," Thag added tersely.

"And when it comes to payin fer the lawyerin," Dave went on, "you ken look to me. And not mention it to the Little Squire."

Lawyer Todd leaned back in his swivel chair. He took off his glasses and laid them on his desk.

"I have already agreed to defend the boy."

"The Old Lady?"

"Not exactly. As a matter of fact, I was expecting Mr. Gwynn when you came in. However, I'm glad you've come." And he glanced more directly at Dave. "Tell me something about the boy. I spent two hours with him last night in his jail cell, but about all I could get out of him was 'Tell Dave Crockett to take care of my horse.'"

Neither Dave nor Thag said anything for a moment. Then Dave said, "I reckon it's jest the way of the Little Squire."

Thag interrupted. "What I want to know is, ken you keep the law from killin Little Squire before his time?"

Richard Todd looked down at his desk. "It'll depend on the evidence. And the kind of jury." He pushed a book toward Thag. "Here's the law—Supreme Court decision— Justice Hogue."

Thag read slowly:

Preparing deadly weapon with intention to use it: Where one person prepares a deadly weapon with intention to use it in case he gets into a fight with another, and goes to a particular place for the purpose of meeting with him and having a conflict with him, and a fight ensues in which that other is killed, the slayer is guilty of murder, because of the preconceived malice, though the deceased first assaulted him with a deadly weapon.

"But Little Squire never prepared a deadly weapon," said Thag angrily, pushing the book aside. "Hit aint like him."

"His pistol was found in the room. We have to face that," Richard Todd said.

"But he never meant to hurt Beldie. He said so."

"I know," and Richard Todd read through the abstract again to himself.

"I'll put up money to bail him out," Thag interrupted.

"Mr. Gwynn has already decided against it. He's afraid if he gets back in those mountains and—"

"Anything wrong with gettin back in the mountains?"

"A forced second arrest might prejudice the court," said Richard Todd evenly.

"But who's to arrest the Little Squire a second time?" Thag insisted. "He never meant to hurt Beldie Thomas. Dave Crockett heard him say so. And that's more law than in a book."

Richard Todd leaned back. "No. It's better to proceed. Judge Spicer, a very clear-minded judge, is sitting. And the prosecuting attorney is new. It'll be his first case."

"What's the new man's name?"

"Prescott. Max Prescott."

"Weren't Dewitt Prescott his daddy?" Thag asked quickly.

178

"Yes."

"How'd a Republican git to be a state lawyer?"

"Young Prescott himself, I understand, voted Democrat last time."

"A Republican turnin against his daddy to git a job?"

"I wouldn't go so far as to say that," Richard Todd answered. "But this will be his first case, and Judge Spicer is an able judge."

"With the law like that," and Thag pointed to the book, his face darkening, "and a Republican defendin the law, I vote fer bailin out the Little Squire."

"Mr. Gwynn—" Richard Todd began, and he turned quickly to Dave. "It'll be a gamble, but there've never been two sets of evidence identical, and no two juries the same. And can you get me someone besides yourself to testify for the boy?"

"How many you want? A hunderd?" Thag asked.

Richard Todd smiled. "No. A few more besides yourself."

Dave stood up. "Hit'll not be hard to find folks from up at the Cove to stand fer the Little Squire."

"Then we have a fighting chance, anyhow."

On the day the trial began, long before sunup, the Cove folk began streaming into Tateboro. They hitched their horses and mules along the streets near the Courthouse. They crowded into the courtroom with set, determined faces. But they were frightened, too, and they sat close-packed and watchful.

179

The clerks, the empty chairs of the jury box, the black robe and dignity of Judge Aaron T. Spicer with his iron-gray hair and thin mouth, awed them. Prescott, the young prosecuting attorney, immediately stirred their resentment. He was short and quick, with a little sandy mustache to make him look older. But he was against Little Squire Jim, and that was enough.

"Taint right to bring the Little Squire to court," they murmured to each other. "Taint right. He's done nothin but maybe kill a man what weren't no more good than a hound dog." They muttered and chewed their tobacco, and shifted uneasily in their seats. "But the Little Squire'll git out somehow. Even ef he has to ride out the door on that hoss of hissen."

Little Jim's horse stood outside, ready. Weeks before the trial they had brought it, tied it under a tree across the street from the jail and in clear view of the barred window. They took turns tending it, one man brushing its coat and feeding it for a whole day. Then another. And Little Jim, standing at the barred window on the third floor, watched. Every day he stood there, motionless. If those tending the horse waved or made some personal gesture, Little Jim apparently took no notice. Yet always they had a feeling that he was looking at the horse, and, sensing that, they took infinite pains with brushing its coat to a bright gloss and stroking its forehead with affection. And as they sat in the court watching the proceedings, they kept thinking, "And he ken ride it home when Lawyer Todd gits him out." They always said that aloud if they could: 'When Lawyer Todd gits him out.' The words sounded sure. But underneath they felt it would

180

almost take the falling of Old Hanging Rock to get Little Squire Jim back home.

When they brought Little Jim into the court, carefully guarded, and led him to a chair beside Lawyer Todd, the Cove folk stirred even more resentfully. "Taint right," they muttered. The boy was wearing a gray-and-yellow checked shirt. "Hit's one of the Big Squire's shirts," Til leaned over to whisper to Dave, "and fillin it out to his daddy's size."

Dave nodded. "But I sure hate to see him growin up before my very eyes like this. I'd a-liked to've kept him jest the way he was."

Til looked away. "Hit's jest like bringin the Big Squire to a court-trial right out of his grave, and that aint right."

"Maybe ef the Big Squire'd—" Dave did not finish.

Back of him a woman was whispering to someone. "Why don't they cut his hair? He'd be handsome. And what strange eyes!" Another woman answered: "I told you you'd be surprised. Harriet said he was the strangest boy she had ever known."

The choice of the jury was a two-day wrangle with Prescott. He was difficult and contentious. Finally Lawyer Todd snapped, "If the prosecution cannot agree on a jury in this county, I shall petition a removal of the case to an adjoining county." Prescott flushed. The selection of the jury moved more speedily to a conclusion.

After a few preliminaries, Prescott called Sheriff Taylor to the witness stand. Sheriff Taylor knew what was expected of him, and his story was simple and direct.

"Did the prisoner resist arrest?" Prescott asked.

"No."

"Did he know why you were at his door?"

"He didn't seem to be surprised."

Prescott then called for the pistol found in the Thomas house. The shirt. The shoes. The bullet.

"Is this the bullet extracted from the heart of the deceased?"

"Yes."

"Is it the same make as those remaining in the pistol?"

"Yes."

"Now, about the pistol. Were there fingerprints of the prisoner on the barrel?"

"Yes."

He handed the sheriff the pistol. "Would you read the carved initials to the jury?"

"J.B."

"For James Boyden?"

"Possibly."

Prescott paused a moment. Then he said, "I turn the witness over to the defense."

Lawyer Todd stirred lazily. "I have no questions at the present time."

There was a slight rustle in the audience.

"Maybe Lawyer Todd's waitin fer Prescott to play his hand," Dave whispered to Til Umbarger. "Lawyer Todd's seen court-trials before."

"But . . ." Til's voice was querulous.

"Order in the court," Judge Spicer snapped, his gavel hitting the bench. Til fell back into his seat.

Prescott called one witness after another. The pattern against Little Jim began to fill out. The hearts of the Cove folk grew heavy. And still Prescott moved on, amassing every bit of official detail he could, calling and recalling the state officers to the stand, until it seemed that only Hesterlee Thomas was left. Then he abruptly said,

"I'd like the court to summon Ephram J. Caskey, local merchant, to the stand."

The Cove folk were startled. Not one of them except Dave Crockett had ever seen the man.

Prescott's face showed gratification at his surprise move. "Your name is Ephram Caskey, is it not?" he began, almost the moment Caskey was in his chair.

"That's it. Ephram J. Caskey, antique furniture and glass at bargain prices."

"How long have you resided in Tateboro?"

"Fifteen years. Buy up old furniture and refinish it myself."

"Do you know the accused?" Prescott asked.

Ephram glanced toward Jim, then back to Prescott. "I do. And he's a killer."

"Why do you say he's a killer?" Prescott pursued quickly.

"He tried to kill me in that house of his up there in the Valley."

The Cove folk gasped. Dave Crockett turned to Thag Totten, but Thag was already on his feet, his face flushed in anger. "What were you," he shouted, pointing his finger at Caskey, "a-doin in the Little Squire's house?"

Judge Spicer lifted his gavel and brought it down on the bench. "Auditors are not permitted to question the witness on the stand."

"But he's a liar ef he says the Little Squire's a killer."

"The gentleman will be seated," Judge Spicer ordered sharply, "or leave the court."

"But what was he a-doin in Little Squire's house?" Thag insisted.

Judge Spicer brought the gavel down on the bench with a violent stroke. "The court orders the gentleman to withdraw from the courtroom. At once."

Thag hesitated for a moment. Then with offended dignity he made his way over the knees of those in seats near him and went through the glass doors. The court waited. Finally, when the doors had swung closed, Prescott said:

"I'll ask Mr. Caskey the same question. What were you doing in the accused's house?"

"It was a cold day and getting dark and I wanted to warm my hands," Ephram answered.

"Tell the court the details."

"Just knocked on the door of the house up there," Caskey began. "In that valley. And I asked to set by the fire to warm my hands. But I hardly set in a chair when he come at me."

"What do you mean—'come at you'?"

"Like I say. I looked up, and there he was coming at me from the side. Before I could say or do anything he had me on the floor. Then he grabbed that pistol, the one on that table there."

"Did you offer any resistance?"

"No, sir. I ran to my truck. But he come after me, shooting and yelling."

"Did any of the bullets hit you?"

"One of em hit a tire, and one passed over my head. But he'd got me if my truck hadn't took me out of that valley in a hurry."

"I rest," Prescott said quickly.

184

"Does the defense wish to question the witness?" Judge Spicer asked.

"I have no questions at the present time," Lawyer Todd answered, glancing at the jury.

Ephram Caskey stepped down from the witness platform.

Prescott began moving a few papers on his desk. He glanced around the room. The atmosphere in the room grew tense. The Cove folk held their breath. Then Prescott nodded to the bailiff.

"Hesterlee Thomas called to the witness stand," the bailiff intoned.

Hesterlee stood up quickly and passed through the gate and up to the platform. She seated herself in the chair, taking off her hat. Her hair fell in a copper mass over her shoulders. She began her story, under Prescott's leading. She talked rapidly, then hesitantly, as if she had been told what she must say and not say. If what she said were true or untrue no one could tell by watching Little Jim's face. He sat by Lawyer Todd, his eyes on Hesterlee's hair, but as she told her story, his hands moved gently over the top of the table in front of him. But when she stepped down from the stand, tearful, pale, distraught, he sat immovable. And from that moment until two days before the end of the trial he did not move a muscle, so far as anyone in the court could determine.

Lawyer Todd began his defense. It was the second week of the trial. He had heard the prosecution's evidence, and he knew better how to build the defense. And he built slowly and carefully. One character witness followed another—Dave Crockett, Thag Totten, Will Hollister, Lew Campbell. During their testimony Little Jim still sat unmoved, detached, as if nothing about it all had anything to do with him. However, for a moment when Til Umbarger burst out, under Prescott's mocking cross-examination, "And ef Little Squire were flyin the mountains, how ken he be killin a man at the same time?" those near Little Jim were sure they saw a smile cross his eyes. Just for a moment. No more.

"And just what time was this that you saw the defendant leaping these great mountain abysses?" Prescott asked, his voice dry.

"I don't tote a watch," answered Til. "I have other ways of knowin day and night time."

"But you said the moon was high. How high?"

"Clear enough to see plain as day."

"Was Sirius in the sky?" Prescott pursued.

"The which?"

"The red star, the fever star."

"No. Hit had lost itself behind the mountain."

"Well, and the next day you saw the prisoner's clothing lying on the rock?"

"Uhhuh."

Judge Spicer interrupted. "Answer 'yes' or 'no.'"

"Yes."

"Did you yourself cross this abyss to examine the clothes?"

"No. Aint nobody but Little Squire could git on that Rock and git back without makin it fall."

"He seems to be an unusual boy, in your mind. Flying over the mountains from cliff to crag."

"He's not like us folks," Til answered, "but they's nothin wrong with him. I've knowed him a long time."

"How long?"

"Long enough to know he aint killin Beldie Thomas."

"Would you think it natural to fly from that rock, say about nine o'clock, when the dog star was setting behind the mountain, and land in Beldie Thomas' house at about ten o'clock?"

"Some things don't go by watch time," Til answered.

"If clothes on a rock and horse hoof marks on a cliff mean he's been in one place, I suppose his shoes and pistol and a shirt found in the room with the dead man, and hoof marks outside, might make you think he had been there, too, wouldn't they?"

Prescott then picked up the shirt found in the Thomas cabin and held it toward Til. "Recognize this?"

"That's the Big Squire's shirt. I've seen him wear it more times than one," Til defended.

Prescott then put the shirt beside Little Jim's shirt. They were the same in size and color, large across the shoulders, gray-and-yellow-checked.

"Am I to understand," Prescott went on, "that this boy's father, the Big Squire as you call him, who has been dead for ten or more years, might have risen from his grave and left his shirt in the Thomas home on the night of the murder?"

"I wouldn't put it past the Big Squire, not fer a minute," Til answered, so quickly that Prescott found himself stupidly asking,

"What's that?"

"They's two different shirts, aint they? Jest as much

187

sense to sayin the Big Squire did it as sayin the Little Squire thought about killin a man and then did it. Some things a man knows aint by watch time, nor law time. And some things that git done aint by watch time nor law time neither."

Prescott's glance swept the judge and the jury, and into the crowded courtroom. "Maybe the witness wouldn't see a dead man lying on the floor if his watch had stopped running." He smiled at his own turn of Til's words.

Lawyer Todd stirred. "Your Honor," he interrupted, "I dislike to object to the prosecuting attorney's procedure, but the excitement of his initial case in this court should not permit him to exercise his personal attitudes at the expense of the witness."

"The point is within the observance of the bench," Judge Spicer said.

When Til returned to his seat Annie whispered, "I'm glad you brung out that about it might have been the Big Squire all the time."

"He had me in a corner fer a minute about the Big Squire gitten up out of his grave," Til admitted.

"You never saw the Big Squire put in his grave, did you?"

"No."

"Then don't let a little sparrer lawyer git you in a corner. How'd he know it wont the Big Squire? Hit might've been."

The trial moved on. Lawyer Todd called the state's officers back to the stand.

"Were the fingerprints of the deceased Beldie Thomas also on the pistol?"

"Not on the barrel."

"On the handle?"

"The fingerprints on the handle and metal adjoining are so confused it is impossible to identify them."

"Then the fingerprints on the handle and metal adjoining could not be declared those of the defendant, James Braxton Boyden, alone, could they?"

"No."

He called Hesterlee Thomas back to the witness stand. "Did the defendant give you those chairs in your house?"

"Yes."

"Did he give you the dishes with the Boyden crest on them?"

"Yes."

"Did he give you that ring with the ruby stone you are now wearing?"

"Yes."

"Did he give you that pistol which was found in your house?"

"No." And her eyes went wide in terror.

"Are you sure?"

"I knew you'd try to say I killed Beldie," she cried. "But I didn't. I didn't. I didn't do it, I tell you."

"When you lit the lamp," Lawyer Todd went on relentlessly, "you said the defendant's arms were around your husband."

"Yes."

"Did you hear the thud of the pistol on the floor before you lit the lamp or after?"

"Before. No, after."

"Which?"

189

"I don't know. Oh, I don't know. I didn't have nothin to do with it, I tell you. Jim brought the pistol. He said he brought the pistol so Beldie could kill him. But it didn't turn out that way. I didn't have nothin to do with it." She had half-risen from the chair, her eyes wild. "I caint stand this. I caint stand this."

Little Jim, who had sat motionless for days, suddenly stirred. "Hesterlee didn't hurt Beldie!" The words cut through the courtroom. Little Jim had risen, and he was looking angrily at Lawyer Todd. "Hesterlee never hurt Beldie!" he shouted again.

"The testimony of the defendant will be accepted when he takes the stand," Judge Spicer interrupted.

"It is not the intention of the defense to ask the prisoner to take the stand," Lawyer Todd said, flushing.

"But perhaps the prisoner could enlighten the court further by taking the stand," Prescott baited. There was a smile of derision in his eyes.

Lawyer Todd turned toward Prescott and looked as if he would reply, but thought better of it. Then he turned to Judge Spicer. "The defense merely stands upon the prerogative that an accused man does not have to take the chair unless he wishes to do so."

"Then I would suggest that the prisoner remain silent unless he speaks from the chair," said Judge Spicer. "Proceed with the witness in the chair."

"I ask for a recess," said Lawyer Todd.

"Recess granted," said Judge Spicer.

That night Lawyer Todd and Dave Crockett held council. "The boy himself has never told me anything. Just one statement: 'I never meant to hurt Beldie.' And on that I've had to build my case—and on what the prosecution has revealed."

Dave listened in silence. Finally he said, "I'm thinkin maybe after what he said today he might speak a word or two about it hisself."

"You mean you think you could get him to talk?"

Dave looked toward the window. "I jest might."

"Then let's go over to see him this minute."

"No," Dave said, "I'd better go jest myself. Maybe in the dark. And jest me and him." He stood up. "I'll come back after awhile."

Two hours later Richard Todd heard Dave's footsteps on the stairs. When he came into the office he eagerly asked, "Did you get him to talk?"

Dave put his hat on the desk and sat down. "Hit took a long time."

"What did he tell?"

Dave looked down at his shoes. "I give my word to him I wouldn't use it on the stand. None of it."

Lawyer Todd's face fell. "Didn't he say anything we—"

"He said Ephram Caskey told him it were me that sent Caskey to his house. And what the boy says and what Caskey told on the stand aint the same." Dave looked away from Lawyer Todd. "Seem like the boy don't want to help hisself. He's frettin more about a little table he's got up there in that house than he is about hisself. He told me where to find it and what to do with it." Dave's voice trailed off.

The lawyer did not interrupt. He knew Dave would tell what he could and no more. "And he kept mentionin the readin of the book, and how the little foxes kept wantin to come close to him," Dave went on vaguely.

"What book?"

Dave shifted in his chair. "Hit were one somebody give him. Jest for him, he kept sayin. Seem like hit was stayin close to his heart that once somebody had give him somethin. Jest fer him. Hit never come in mind that he ever wanted anybody or anything close to him."

Lawyer Todd shifted the books on his desk. "Did he tell you anything," he asked slowly, "about the night of the killing? Anything, I mean, that you can tell?"

"Hit were like Til said. He did ride to the Rock first."

"Yes?"

"And hit's like that woman said," he finally broke out. "He took the gun."

"I know that. But why?"

"He said he reckoned he was goin to git killed sometime, anyhow."

"Yes?"

"And he put on the shirt, fer he said hit weren't fitten fer a Boyden to git killed without a shirt on."

Lawyer Todd rose and went to the window. "There isn't anything more you could tell in court?"

"No," Dave answered. "I give my word. And hit's not fer me to say what's in the Little Squire's mind to do. He kept repeatin he's mighty beholden to the folks fer takin care of his hoss and things."

Outside, the lights along the dark street were bright, but the trees on the Courthouse lawn were black. "Suppose. Just suppose we put him on the stand anyhow," Lawyer Todd said.

192

"You'd have to do the askin," Dave answered quickly. "And whatever he says on the stand will be to yore doin. But I never met the man or woman that knowed how that boy's mind was turnin, or gonna turn."

"But maybe on the stand . . ." Lawyer Todd continued, as if debating more with himself than with Dave.

"Then you'll have to go yoreself to the askin," Dave answered.

"I'll go over now."

Outside, Dave left Lawyer Todd and rejoined the Cove folk. He told them little, only that Lawyer Todd was going to see the boy and that Lawyer Todd was going to ask him to go on the stand himself. He did tell, though, what Jim had said about their taking care of the horse. At that, Til's face brightened, and excitedly he burst out, "Hit's clear to me, even ef it aint to you. He's goin on the stand and there's no tellin what he's aimin to do. And I'm gonna keep the hoss ready to fly. Ready to fly."

The next morning they brought the horse and tied it under the tree an hour earlier than usual. They left its strap looser. They drew lots again to see who would have to stay outside, "keepin the hoss ready, ef the Little Squire takes it into his head to do somethin except let the court-trial keep turnin against him." Their excitement spread along the streets. The townspeople, caught up in the possibility of some new turn in the trial, crowded into the courtroom, lining the walls when there were no more seats, and filling the vestibule outside.

But Richard Todd did not call Little Jim to the stand during the morning session. He seized upon every detail to

193

delay the court. He called Ephram Caskey back to the witness chair.

"You said previously that the defendant shot at you and hit the tire of your truck?" Lawyer Todd asked.

"Yes."

"Do you still have the tire?"

"No."

"Then you have no evidence that what you say is the truth?"

"I'm not lying on the witness stand."

Lawyer Todd nodded. Then he asked, almost diffidently, "And how long were you in the defendant's house, trying to buy some of his furniture?"

"Close to half an hour. Maybe an hour."

"Did he take you upstairs in Little Stepper House?"

"No. Just in that long big front room. The one with the pictures."

Lawyer Todd paused and turned to the clerk. "Will the clerk reread Caskey's previous testimony relative to his arrival at the house?"

The clerk turned back and began reading: "Witness Caskey: 'It was a cold day and getting dark, and I wanted to warm my hands.' Prescott, prosecution: 'Tell the court the details.' Witness Caskey: 'I just knocked on the door of the house up there in the Valley and asked to set by the fire, and I hadn't hardly set in a chair when he come at me.' "

"That's enough," Lawyer Todd interrupted, and turned back to Caskey, who was mopping his brow. "Which is the court to believe?" he shot at him.

"It was like I said," Caskey burst out. "He shot at me."

"But which is the court to believe? An hour? Or just enough time to go in and sit down?"

Caskey looked helplessly at Prescott.

"I release the witness," said Lawyer Todd abruptly. "I'll raise the question of perjury at another time"; and he turned away from Caskey.

He recalled other witnesses. The morning was passing. But he did not call Hesterlee Thomas back to the stand. Twelve o'clock came, and still he had not called Little Jim to the stand.

At one-thirty the court reconvened.

A few minutes after two o'clock the sergeant-at-arms stood up. "James Braxton Boyden to the witness chair."

Little Jim stood up. He went toward the witness platform. He stepped upon the stand and turned to face the room. His eyes were blue and yellow-flecked. There was a dignified calmness about his every move, and this calmness seemed to throw a hypnotic spell over the room, and in the breathless pause as he stood up there in front of them on the platform the Cove folk thought of Amelia Boyden's funeral, when the winds were high to mingle with the words of the priest and the rattle of Old Lady Gwynn's rosary, and Little Jim standing at the head of his mother's grave, his feet wide, that suggestion of animal grace about his body, his red hair wild in the wind; and when they shook their heads, he was gone . . .

Lawyer Todd cleared his throat. In a voice low and persuasive he said: "Let's begin at the beginning. Your name is James Braxton Boyden, isn't it?"

The clock on the wall ticked out ten seconds before Little Jim finally nodded.

"Answer 'yes' or 'no,'" ordered Judge Spicer.

"I beg Your Honor's pardon," Lawyer Todd interrupted, "but I should like permission to do this in my own way."

"The defendant should answer verbally," insisted Judge Spicer. "However, for the present, proceed."

Little Jim turned and looked at Judge Spicer, then back over the heads of the audience. The blueness of his eyes had not changed.

"And you live in Little Stepper Valley?" Lawyer Todd went on. "And in this valley lie buried your father, your grandfather, your great-grandfather, and his father before him?"

"About."

The sound of that one word was startling. Almost as startling as if the boy had suddenly disappeared from the room, sprung on his horse, and actually flown off.

"And how did these meet their deaths?"

"Killed."

Lawyer Todd's relief showed in his face. "How old are you?" he went on.

The boy's eyes turned suddenly dark. He glanced out the window.

"Are you seventeen? or eighteen?"

There was no answer. Lawyer Todd looked at his notes for a moment. He put them in his pocket. "Well, then, Jim. Let's begin at the main point. You have heard the testimony in the court of the state's officers, of Ephram Caskey, and of Hesterlee Thomas. Now you tell your side of the story."

Little Jim turned his shoulders slightly. He looked down

196

at Lawyer Todd, and then toward the corner where Hester-lee was sitting, her fingers nervously twisting a heavily jeweled ring. Her eyes fell. Little Jim turned back.

"Then, Jim, begin where you rode up on your horse and the deceased and his wife invited you to come into the house."

Prescott interrupted. "I object to the leading of the witness."

"Objection overruled," intoned Judge Spicer. "These are only facts known to the court through previous testimony."

"Then I shall petition the same liberty of procedure," Prescott said.

Judge Spicer looked at him sternly. "The bench attempts always to be impartial."

Prescott flushed. "I beg Your Honor's pardon."

Lawyer Todd moved closer to Little Jim. He spoke low, almost with pleading in his voice. "Then tell the court, Jim, how after an agreement to be allowed to talk to his wife, the deceased returned with your pistol in his hand."

Judge Spicer leaned across his desk and said impatiently: "The court asks that you tell the details of that night. Certain points need to be cleared up. At least assist your own lawyer in your defense."

Little Jim turned and looked at Judge Spicer. "I'm up here just to favor Dave Crockett."

"I release the witness to the prosecution," Lawyer Todd said abruptly.

Prescott, momentarily caught off his guard by the suddenness of Lawyer Todd's move, sprang to his feet. His youth, his leanness, his shortness, his sharp eyes and sandy mustache perched insolently on his upper lip made him all of a piece, and his nervousness did not soften the biting edge of his voice. Little Jim looked down at him.

"You say your name is James Braxton Boyden? And you have lived all your life in Little Stepper Valley, of this county?" And with no pretense of waiting for an answer, he rushed on. "You took the pistol to the Thomas house to use it if he refused to let you sleep with his wife, didn't you?"

The crowd in the courtroom was startled at the directness of the question. They held their breath, their eyes steady on the face of the boy.

"And you forced the deceased at the point of that pistol to leave the house? Didn't you wilfully rape the deceased's wife? Didn't you—"

"I object," Lawyer Todd shouted, springing to his feet. "The prosecution is trying to force an erroneous admission from the prisoner."

"Objection overruled," replied Judge Spicer. And then he added drily, "No one seems to have led the witness to admit anything up to the present time, so far as I can see."

A nervous titter went through the room.

"Didn't you attack the deceased in his own house?" Prescott drove on, reckless in his wording. "Didn't you force a fight and shoot him? Didn't you then, appalled at your own murderous deed, mount your horse and ride away?"

Lawyer Todd sprang to his feet. "I object, Your Honor. The prosecution's lack of experience in court cannot excuse the irregularity of his remarks. I shall petition for a mistrial if he continues in such a vein."

The two lawyers glowered at each other. For a moment the issue of Little Jim Boyden's guilt was forgotten. It had become merely a personal contest between the two men. Little Jim looked down upon them. A smile passed over his face, and then in a detached drawl he said, almost gently, as if to pacify the two men,

"I never meant to hurt Beldie."

"What do you mean by *hurt*?" Prescott whipped out. "Kill? You mean you never meant to kill Beldie Thomas?"

The Cove folk drew in their breath in terrible fear. They clung to Little Jim's face.

Then Little Jim nodded.

It was no more than that—a nod—but to the Cove folk it was as if they stood far below and suddenly had seen Hanging Rock shiver, teeter on the ledge, and then bend forward to fall. A moan broke from them.

"Order in the court," Judge Spicer barked, striking the bench with his gavel.

But Prescott, with a flash of genius, caught the moment. "Now that the witness has admitted on the stand in the open court that he killed the deceased, Beldie Thomas, I rest."

He sat down.

The room broke into an uproar. "Order in the court. Order in the court," Judge Spicer pounded. Hesterlee Thomas tried to stand up. Lawyer Todd went to the judge's desk. The excitement running through the room reached the jury. Some of them half-stood up, not knowing what they meant to do. Judge Spicer pounded the desk. "Order in the court," he shouted.

In all the excitement only Little Jim seemed completely

unperturbed. He calmly turned his face toward the judge's bench. Nothing more than that. Yet the movement had in it more power than all the pounding of the gavel on the desk. The room grew deathly still.

"Do you wish to say more to the court?" Judge Spicer asked.

Little Jim kept his eyes on him for a moment, then before anyone knew what he was doing, he stepped down from the platform.

For a moment even Judge Spicer was caught unprepared. Then he pulled the threads of procedure together again. "Does the defense have further witnesses to present to the court?" he asked, looking at Lawyer Todd.

"No."

"Then, as the afternoon session is still young, does the prosecution wish to begin the summation of the case for the state?"

The sudden turn of Little Jim's words, the advantages of making use of the confused emotions and implications, prompted Prescott to say: "Yes. The prosecution wishes to proceed immediately to its summation."

"Proceed," Judge Spicer said, surprised himself at Prescott's decision.

Attorney Prescott gathered a few papers from his table and went toward a place in front of the jury. His voice was sharp to an edge. He was flushed. He asked for the abstract of the decision of Justice Hogue in *State versus Jones,* pertaining to preparing a deadly weapon and taking it to a place where a fight ensues. He then began his summary.

He rehearsed the details of the evidence—the state's

200

officials' evidence, Hesterlee's words. He dwelt on Jim's bringing the gun, the forced bargain in the room. Then, from the scattered details of Hesterlee's testimony, he reconstructed the fight. He stepped off the distances, the positions, and came to the death of Beldie Thomas. He wove the details with such vividness and ingenuity that a pall fell over the court. He dwelt upon the most insidious and damning aspects of the testimonies. He caught himself and the court up in his intensity and imagination until suddenly into the midst of his words broke Little Jim's voice, "I never meant to hurt Beldie Thomas, I told you."

Prescott stopped. The suddenness of the interruption startled him.

Judge Spicer raised his gavel. "Do you wish to take the stand again?"

Lawyer Todd turned toward Jim. The court waited. Jim did not move.

"Do you wish to take the stand again?" Judge Spicer repeated.

Still there was no response from Jim.

"Proceed," Judge Spicer said to the prosecution.

Attorney Prescott continued point by point, finishing: "And, gentlemen of the jury, let me point to you again that the prisoner did wilfully and with forethought force himself into the home of this woman, this faithful, helpless wife. These are the facts of the case. There is no confusion of evidence." He turned toward Hesterlee. "Look at her now—pale, trembling, helpless. Her eyes show her distress." He turned back to the jury. "And let me emphasize to you that when this man had glutted himself, he, like a depraved animal, shot her husband. Shot a man. A citizen living in peace. Striving to earn a livelihood across the mountains to support his tender wife."

"Hit's a lie. Hit's a lie." The words rang out. Hesterlee stood up wildly. "Hit's a lie," she cried. "I'm not Beldie's wife. We never married. We jest lived together. And . . ." Judge Spicer tried to interrupt, but Hesterlee cried the faster, "And Beldie was not a good man like he says. Beldie was hidin because he killed a man in Tennessee. He killed the man with a knife."

"Order in the court." The gavel hit the heavy oak of the desk. "Order in the court."

The room grew suddenly still.

"You have given your testimony," Judge Spicer admonished Hesterlee in a stern voice. "The interruption is subject to severe reprimand."

Attorney Prescott shouted with shaken nerves. "I object, Your Honor, to the injection of facts not pertinent to the case. The deceased's previous record has no bearing on this case."

"The jury will be instructed by the bench at the proper time." Judge Spicer's voice was as cold as his eyes on the young attorney.

Attorney Prescott grew confused. He cleared his throat and began again: "And furthermore, I say to you, gentlemen of the jury, that this man sitting here deserves the death penalty for wilfully and with malice aforethought doing to death by murder one Beldie Thomas, and I—"

"But Beldie killed a man in Tennessee," Hesterlee's voice rose in a scream.

"Remove the woman from the courtroom," ordered Judge Spicer, "until she can control herself."

Hesterlee, between two guards, was forced up from her chair.

Lawyer Todd went up quickly to speak to Judge Spicer. He talked excitedly for a moment. Judge Spicer shook his head. Lawyer Todd talked on insistently. The judge shook his head again and opened a book, and with one finger pointed to a passage. Lawyer Todd only glanced at it, and returned to his chair.

"Does the prosecution wish to continue?" Judge Spicer asked.

"I rest," Attorney Prescott answered.

Judge Spicer called Lawyer Todd to the desk. They exchanged a few words. The lawyer nodded.

"Court is recessed until nine o'clock tomorrow morning."

That night Annie Umbarger smoothed her hair carefully, took her bonnet on her arm, and with a nod to her sister Lucy she stepped outside into the dusk. Will Hollister was waiting for her. The children along the road and porches of Anderstown eyed them curiously. They went past the mill, across the railroad tracks, and up Hill Street. When they came to a brown bungalow, the George Hull house, Will stopped. "This is where I let her and her trunk out that time."

"Wait out here till I git back," Annie said, and went up

203

the walk. She knocked on the door. George Hull came to the screen.

"You Mister Hull?" Annie asked, her voice low in sudden shyness at seeing him, a stranger to her, yet someone she must talk to about the Little Squire.

"Yes."

"Could I say a word to the missus, too?"

"She's putting the baby to bed at the moment," he answered, "but won't you come in?" He held the screen open for her.

She went in, awed at the rugs, the heavy overstuffed furniture, the wide doors opening from one room into another.

"Won't you sit here?" he went on, offering her a wing-chair near the fireplace. "I'll call Ellen."

"Jest say hit's Annie Umbarger, from up Crocketts Cove," she said.

She sat down in the big chair, holding her bonnet nervously on her lap, her feet not even touching the floor. Soon she heard someone coming down the steps, and in a moment Ellen Hull entered. She was a pretty woman, in her late twenties, simply dressed, her hair a dark gold loosely caught up into a knot at the back of her neck. Annie tried to struggle from the chair. "I'm Annie Umbarger," she repeated.

"Please don't get up," Ellen answered, seating herself and wondering at Annie's tense eyes.

"Have you been to the trial of the Little Squire?" Annie asked.

"Oh, yes," Ellen answered quickly, grasping the connection in Annie's simple dress and rough shoes and her

204

question. "George and I take turns. And I think I've seen you there."

"Little Squire's ourn, too," Annie answered simply, "and I've come . . ." She hesitated, searching Ellen's face. "I mean, do you reckon . . . I mean, Miss Harriet . . ."

"Oh, then you know Harriet Evans?"

"She were a pretty girl, and she knowed old Annie. And the Little Squire, he . . ."

"Yes," said Ellen, looking down. "She told me a little, just enough for me to guess." She looked up. "And you love him, too?"

"He's ourn," Annie repeated. "And I've come . . . Do you reckon, could you git hold of Miss Harriet and ask her to come to the trial? To come a-hurryin?"

"Come here? At once?"

"The Little Squire won't talk fer hisself," she rushed on, her voice a cry, "and nobody ken do anything. And Miss Harriet always had a way with the Little Squire, in the way of my yeller trillie," and she looked down at her bonnet, "and I got to wonderin and hopin . . ."

"That if she would come, she could get him to talk and tell his side?"

Annie nodded quickly, her hands beginning to tremble.

"But would she have time?" Ellen asked.

"I never figured the time," Annie cried, sudden fear showing in her eyes. "I been jest worryin, but ef you could git her to come, jest come . . ."

"I can get George to send a message at once," Ellen said, glancing toward the stairs. "And if she gets it in time she can come and we'll meet her at Rural Hall."

"Oh, would ye?" Annie slipped out of the chair in her excitement. "I'm leavin to let you git at it fore hit's too late."

"But is that all? Couldn't I—"

But Annie only shook her head frantically. "Jest git Miss Harriet to come and ask him to speak fer hisself, and that's mornin and night and come spring time in the world fer old Annie Umbarger." She was at the door, holding her bonnet clenched. "And heart-feelins to you fer-ever."

"But if I should want to see you again?" Ellen asked, following her to the door.

"I'm stayin with Sister Lucy over in Anderstown."

"Lucy McVay, the granny-woman?"

"That's Sister Lucy," Annie answered, dropping her eyes. "Little Squire's trouble makes us close again in the heart, and nothin to remember that hurts." She gave a sudden bob of her head. "And tell Miss Harriet old Annie is hopin and wantin." She searched Ellen's face again before adding, "And could ye tell her not to let on to the Little Squire hit were old Annie that knows why he fetched my yeller trillie in the night and knows to ask her to come?"

With that she turned and fled across the porch, and Ellen saw her rejoin Will Hollister at the walk.

The next morning Judge Spicer opened court on the minute, and shortly after nine o'clock he asked the counsel for the defense of James Braxton Boyden to proceed with his summary before the jury.

Lawyer Todd arose. Outwardly he was himself again—

206

the slow, easy, the big-brother-who-was-a-lawyer air about his every movement. He held a paper with a few scattered notes on it. The paper was steady in his hand. His voice as he began his summary had a quiet persuasiveness. The court listened in quiet attention to his words.

Little Jim never once moved his eyes from the speaking man.

He summarized the evidence in Little Jim's favor. With extraordinary clarity he pointed out the weaknesses in the state's charges. Then he turned to the more general aspects of the case.

He talked for an hour and a half. It was a moving speech, simple, direct, and logical. "And in the depth of my heart I know," he said finally, "and you in the depths of your hearts know also, that this boy did not have the intention to kill. Nor did he kill. And I ask you to keep the realization of this before you as you study the facts of the case and, in reaching your decision, let the clarity of your hearts as well as the clarity of your heads guide you."

When he sat down Annie looked at Til and nodded her head. She turned around to nod at Old Dave just at her back. But Old Dave was looking at the jury, trying to fathom the expression on their faces. He thought he could discern a gentleness on their faces. But he was not sure.

Judge Spicer asked Lawyer Prescott if he had further words to close the case, or if he waived the privilege.

Attorney Prescott jumped to his feet. Indeed he would not waive the right to close the case. He would not wish the jury to leave the room with a confusion of issues in their minds. He would want them to recall certain phases of the testimony. He would have the law pertaining to the

207

case read again. No? Then it would be read in the charge to the jury? Yes. Anyhow, he would recall to them the doctrine of the law appertaining to the case as handed down by Justice Hogue: 'Where if a weapon is brought for the intent to use it in case of a fight, and a fight ensues, and the death of that other results, murder has been committed.'

"And I ask you," he persisted with the tenacity of a terrier with his teeth in the throat of some larger dog, "what reason would the prisoner have for bringing a pistol, his own pistol—by proof—, to the deceased's house, except for the purpose for which he did use it? I repeat the words *to kill*. Kill a man." He paused for the effect of his argument.

There was not a sound in the court.

"And you have heard the prisoner testify on the witness stand that he 'killed' the man. *Hurt* is the word his counsel would prefer. But *killed* is the word meant, upon admission of the prisoner himself. I ask, therefore," and his voice rose to strident intensity, "for the supreme penalty, sentence to the lethal chamber."

"Is that the same as hangin?" The interruption cut clearly through the room. The words were so sudden that the court could hardly make sure of them. Little Jim had not moved when he asked the question. Yet the voice was his.

"The end is the same," snapped Attorney Prescott.

Little Jim shifted. "Then put me in there," he said slowly. "I'm not afeared of killed."

Swift as the crack of a whip, and as relentlessly, the little attorney cried: "There is your further admission on the part of the prisoner. He not only has admitted he killed the man, but he recognizes his guilt and asks for the death penalty for himself. I have no more to say."

He sat down.

Stifled cries, moans, coughs, movement of bodies in helpless shiftings. The judge glowered at the room, quelling incipient disorder with cold eyes. In the pause Til Umbarger, sitting near the back of the room, got up. He whispered to Annie, a catch in his voice. "I ought to go look at the hoss."

"You want me to go with you?" Annie asked. She was crying silently, her bony little hands moving helplessly.

Til shook his head. "I jest aimed to go see fer myself."

Judge Spicer rose. He gave the charge to the jury. He clarified their duties. He again cited the law. He ordered the bailiff to show the jury out.

The jury stood up. But Little Jim rose also. The jury paused, their eyes upon him.

The prosecuting attorney turned pale. He looked as if he would like to make violent objection. The room was caught in breathless stillness. Finally Little Jim said in a slow drawl, his eyes on the jury, "I'm not afeared of gettin killed."

"The bailiff will show the jury to its room," Judge Spicer sharply ordered.

The jury filed out. Recess was declared.

It was exactly eleven-thirty by the Courthouse clock. The courtroom emptied out onto the lawn in the front.

"Could anybody tell by lookin at the jury the way they're thinkin?" Broat Totten asked, his voice husky.

209

Thag wouldn't answer. He only turned away, walking hurriedly across the lawn.

Annie Umbarger opened up a box of food. She spread it out along the rear brace of the memorial cannon on the lawn. She took off her bonnet and smoothed back her hair. She had baked a cake "into the middle of the night." And early before five she had caught a chicken and fried it. "Dave Crockett, have a breast of chicken," she urged. "And come on here, Til, and eat."

"I aint hongry."

"Eat a bite, anyhow. Don't do Little Jim any good not to eat, leastways after I stayed up half the night to fix it."

"I aint got taste fer nothin this minute," Til insisted.

"I aint askin you have you got a taste," Annie said. "Jest eat a bite." She put a piece of chicken in his hand, and a biscuit.

"Little Squire Jim aint got no sense sayin that to the jury."

Annie busied herself about the food. "Here, Dave Crockett, try a pickle." In a moment she said to Til, "I've been knowin Little Squire long as anybody, and aint nobody knows what's goin on in his head."

Til burst out: "Old Lady Gwynn herself ought to do somethin fer Little Jim. She could come ridin into town an do somethin."

Annie cut him a slice of cake. "Here, eat some of this."

"Maybe when she hears how things is goin with Little Squire she'll wild-ride in an do somethin," Til insisted.

Old Dave swallowed in silence. After a time Annie began putting the remains of the lunch together. "Caint never tell what Little Squire'll be thinkin an doin. Caint never tell. Wait and see. . . ." Her words were desperately cheerful. "Keep that there hoss of hissen untied and ready, Til."

But at four o'clock the jury was still out.

"Maybe they're waitin fer Old Lady Gwynn to ride in an do somethin," Til suggested hopefully.

"Maybe she don't know about it," answered Annie.

Til looked away. He felt uneasy at the words. Go down to where the Gwynns live? Ask her to do something? "I wouldn't mind gitten on Old Hangin Rock, ef the moon was right," he said, "but I aint up to that."

Annie's face was pinched. Under her bonnet her eyes had lost their glint. They looked gray and faded like her face. And at five o'clock she suddenly said: "I got to be goin back to the Cove and holdin things together. Every muscle inside me is beginnin to shake and tremble. You men folks'll have to run things. Hit'll be dark now, fore I git home." She left the food with Til. "Eat, anyhow," she insisted. "And keep that hoss breshed and fixed." She strode off through the Saturday crowd that filled the sidewalks in front of the stores.

At nine o'clock the jury was still locked.

The next morning the church bells were ringing. "Ef somethin don't take a turn," Til said moodily to Dave Crockett, "I'm aimed to go down and speak to Old Lady Gwynn, ef I die lookin at her."

"Reckon you caint meddle with folks when hit's their folks," Old Dave answered. "Taint fitten."

They looked up to the jail window. Jim's face was staring down from the barred opening. Since early morning he had been there, his hands on the bars, motionless. The eyes were on the stallion. Early Thag Totten had curried it, brushed the coat with lingering care, walked it up and down, before tying it under the tree in full view of the window. Little groups of townspeople going to and from Sunday school or church stopped to gaze at it, fascinated by its wild strength. Unconsciously, too, they found themselves fascinated by the somber eyes and copper hair behind the bars in the high jail window. But the crowds shifted and changed, and melted away, leaving only the stallion and the boy above, his hands tight upon the bars as if he would break them in his grip.

And at one o'clock the jury had its dinner sent into them on trays.

But about two-thirty Til, sitting under the tree, saw Jim's head turn. Eldo's ears pointed forward. Til sprang up.

Far down the street the faint clatter of horses' hoofs was breaking the Sunday stillness. Til's heart jumped. Old Lady Gwynn's carriage was coming toward Courthouse Square. He could see it. He could see the horses, heads reined high, in fast pace; Waldo on the box, coachman's hat gleaming in the sun; Julia Gwynn in black feathers and lace parasol sitting stiffly in the back seat. "Old Lady Gwynn's comin to help out Little Jim. She's comin to help Little Jim," flashed through Til's mind. "She's goin to stop at the Courthouse. She's goin to stop."

But the carriage was not stopping. It was passing. It was out of sight. Maybe it hadn't happened. Til looked vacantly around. The bay stallion stood close by. Little

212

Jim was in the window, high above, hands gripping the bars. Til shook his head. Yet, far down Hill Street he could hear a fading clatter of the hoof beats. And then nothing.

Til ran across to the Courthouse lawn. The Campbell boys and Broat Totten had been sitting over there. They were now standing. Yes, they had seen her. Yes, but she didn't stop. Maybe she didn't know. They held a council. "Broat, run down Hill Street and see where her carriage is stoppin."

Broat started off in a brisk run. Soon he was back.

"Her hosses is hitched in front of Dr. Will Snowe's. She's in the house, and that nigger's settin up there on the carriage waitin for her to come back out."

"When she comes back we'll stop her," Til cried. "And you, Ancil, git down the street toward Dr. Snowe's house and holler to Parry when you see her comin. And you, Parry, you holler up to Broat, and then we'll all git ready and stop her."

They flew to their posts. They waited. They hardly felt the half-hour of waiting.

Soon they heard Ancil's shout far down Hill Street, and another, and Broat Totten near the corner yelled: "She's comin up the street. She comin hell-splittin."

The clatter of the hoofs on the paved street rang through the trees. Til ran out into the street. The carriage turned the corner. Til was almost in the path of the horses. He shouted. The others shouted.

But the carriage swerved. Waldo tapped the horses to stretch out their broken pace. Til, Ancil, Thag—all of them shouted. But the carriage was passing, was going down the street; and they could only turn and stare help-lessly at each other, hearing the clatter and grinding of wheels losing themselves down the street.

Til turned to Willie Vaughn. "Run to the house where Old Dave's takin a nap and wake him up. Tell him Old Lady Gwynn rode by an done nothin fer Little Jim. Tell him to step over and tell us what we're to do." He looked up to the window.

Back of them the bay stallion pawed. Its ears were pointed forward, its eyes, wide and eager, were on Jim's window. It pawed again. Little Jim seemed to grip the iron bars tighter. And yet it seemed, too, that he had not moved.

Old Dave came. He shook his head sadly. "He's her folks. And folks like us caint meddle. He's her folks."

Til looked up to the boy in the window and cried help-lessly. "Looks like he's aimin to break them bars hisself, and quit foolin around."

E L D O

That Sunday night George and Ellen returned from Rural Hall with Harriet Evans. Her train had been late and it was almost ten o'clock when they finally reached home. Harriet had talked of Little Jim all the way home.

"I went to see Judge Spicer myself," Ellen said, "and he told me if the boy would talk or in any way throw some new light on the case, he'd agree to a new trial. The jury's been out since yesterday morning, and there must be some-

215

thing not clear even in their own minds. But you'll have to get him to talk before court convenes in the morning. You'll just have to."

"Couldn't I go and see him tonight?" Harriet insisted. "I know he didn't kill that man. He couldn't."

But when George called up the office of the jail he was told that it was closed for the night to all visitors. "You'll have to wait until morning," he had to tell her. "But the jury is still hung up," he added. "That gives you time."

"I'll have early breakfast and you can see him in the morning before court opens," Ellen suggested. "Come on up now, darling," she urged, "and get a good bath. A day on a train is a long time."

"And in the morning I'll go with you myself to see him," George said.

But at this suggestion Harriet shook her head quickly.

"Don't you want George to go with you?" Ellen asked.

"I'd want him," Harriet answered, "but I don't think I could get Little Jim to talk if anybody were with me."

"Then you do it your own way, dear." And she put her arms around Harriet. "Come along to bed now. It'll be easier tomorrow."

The next morning Harriet was up early. The night's rest had given her cheeks a renewed glow, but her gray eyes showed her anxiety. Immediately after breakfast she started toward the Courthouse.

Harriet hurried up the street. When she turned the corner at the Square and caught sight of Little Jim's horse and the Cove folk, she gasped. "Oh, I never thought they'd bring Eldo. And there's Til Umbarger." She ran toward them. She greeted them. Thag Totten, Dave

216

Crockett, Til. They were overjoyed to see her. And surprised.

"Annie's been a-sayin and a-sayin," Til said wistfully, "ef only you'd come."

"I came as soon as I heard. But where's Annie?"

"She come to the trial as long as she could," Til answered, "but she went back Saturday to hold things together, she said, at home, so I ken stay and tend to Little Squire's hoss. But," and there was a sudden catch in his voice, "I had a feelin she were afeared she'd hear somethin she'd not want to hear ef she stayed."

Under the tree the stallion grew suddenly restive. It nickered and scraped the street with its front hoof. Its ears pointed toward Harriet.

"Why, I believe he remembers me!" Harriet cried, and impulsively put her hand up to smooth Eldo's forehead and neck. The stallion tossed its head at her caress.

"Hit's a sign," Til burst out. "He's not let anybody tech him like that since Little Squire's been up there."

Harriet's hand on the horse trembled. "I'm going to talk to Little Jim now," she said, so low that if Til had not been so close to her shoulder he could not have heard her.

"Then tell the Little Squire," he whispered, "we're keepin him untied and standin ready, so he ken git right on him and fly off to the mountains, when he calls."

Harriet made no answer. She didn't want them to see that she was crying. Without turning she hurried across the street toward the jail.

John Moore was in his office. In his quiet old eyes he carried the variables of hundreds of human struggles with the law. He was quiet, but he was watchful. The years had

217

made him so. He had been jailer when the Llewellens from over Low Gap way had mustered their whole clan, ridden into Tateboro and surrounded the Courthouse and jail. He had been there long before that too, when one of the McGaws had hanged himself in his cell.

At Harriet's knock he glanced up.

"I'd like to talk to Jim Boyden, just a little while," she began.

"You some of his family?"

"No. But I knew him back in the mountains."

"It's almost time to get the prisoner ready for court," he hesitated. "Judge Spicer's sent word that court's going to open at the stroke of nine."

"But Judge Spicer told Ellen Hull I could talk with him, before," Harriet pleaded.

John Moore eyed her, still uncertain. "It's not a safe thing to do. We just don't go close to him, except to slip a tray under his door. And he's not touched a bite of food for a week or more."

"But I'm not afraid of him," Harriet cried. "And Judge Spicer said—"

John Moore wavered. He didn't want anything to happen. He would be blamed. That big stallion out there. The guards had been doubled.

"And I've traveled almost two whole days," Harriet cried. "And Judge Spicer says if I can get him to tell his side, or promise, he'll declare a mistrial."

"All right," John Moore said abruptly. "I'll go with you myself. Maybe . . . Jest maybe . . ." He looked at her sadly. "I knowed the Big Squire in his day, and it's heavy on my heart to have his boy up there. Sometimes

218

I've almost wished . . ." He glanced out the window toward the stallion. "We'll have to hurry," he said, taking a key from the box.

He led the way down the hall, then up a narrow flight of steps, then another, until they came to the third floor, and then down a corridor lined with cells. When he came to the one in the front corner, he stopped. "He's in there."

Harriet looked through the bars. He was sitting on the floor, eyes down. He seemed to have grown since she had last seen him. His head seemed more massive, his shoulders broader. And yet there was about him still that deep brownness of sun and that strangeness that made her emotions fly back to the night in the mountains with the sound of the cascade in the distance, the pale trilliums about the pool, and his voice whispering, 'I fetched it just for you.' . . .

"A young lady to see you," John Moore said, breaking through her thoughts, bringing her back to the bars, the cell, and Jim sitting in there on the floor.

He did not move even to look up.

"I've come, Jim."

At the sound of her voice he lifted his head.

"I came as soon as I heard," Harriet rushed on, struggling to quiet the emotion in her voice. "I wanted to come."

Little Jim swiftly rose from the floor. His eyes were dark. Harriet grasped the bars to steady herself. For a moment the white walls and bars were a nothingness about him. He was standing there before her, free of everything, his hands hanging loosely down, his eyes dark to a blackness on her.

219

"I'm mighty proud you came."

"I wanted to come to help you when I heard," she cried.

"You didn't keep your promise," he interrupted.

"My promise?"

"That time."

"Oh." Confusion swept over her. "But I couldn't, Jim. That time. I thought you'd forgotten."

"You promised."

"I couldn't keep my promise, Jim. Mr. Hollister sat in the yard watching me. And the next day I had to leave. And they wouldn't let me come back to the Cove. But I've come back now, Jim. And I want you to tell them you didn't kill that man. Just tell them."

"I've been keepin somethin for you," he interrupted.

"But Judge Spicer says if you'll tell—"

"It's in the room up in the top of my house. Under some things. It's just a . . ." He paused as if uncertain. "A little table. And in the drawers are some things." He paused again, a fleeting smile in his eyes. "Lessen the foxes got in to eat them."

"But Jim," Harriet tried to interrupt. "Tell them you didn't kill that man."

"Old Dave said he'd get it for you," he went on as if she were not talking. "I kept it for you."

"That's . . . that's . . ." she stumbled. "Of course, Jim, and I'll keep it. I want it because you want to give it to me. I'll keep it always—"

"I asked Old Dave last night to get it for you."

"But Jim," she cried, grasping the bars until her knuckles were white. "We haven't much time. Judge

220

Spicer said if you'll tell your side, he'll call the jury back. He'll have a new trial. He'll—"

"I don't want a new trial."

"But you didn't kill that man. I know you didn't."

His hands moved slightly. Then he said quietly, "I'm not afeared."

"But they'll put you in that room. You'll be killed."

He shifted. He seemed to grow taller. His eyes grew darker. For a moment it seemed the walls could not hold him. Then, "I'm not afeared of killed."

"But you don't know what you're saying!" she cried.

"I'm not afeared of bein killed," he repeated tonelessly.

Harriet turned to John Moore. "He keeps saying words over and over. He doesn't know what he's saying."

John Moore's eyes were on Little Jim. "Yes," he breathed, "he knows what he's saying."

Little Jim moved one hand slightly. "I never meant to hurt Beldie," he said, "but—" and his hand moved again slightly.

"Oh," she sobbed, falling back. "Then . . ." She could not finish.

"I'm mighty proud you came," he said slowly.

From down the corridor hurried a man. He was breathless and excited. "The court's opened. And Judge Spicer is waiting. And the jury's back in the courtroom." He glanced at Harriet.

Two guards were coming down the corridor. They were large fellows and one of them was carrying a pair of handcuffs. They reached Jim's door. They looked with surprise

221

at Harriet. One of them unlocked the cell door and held it half-ajar. "We're gonna slip these on today, young feller."

He rattled the handcuffs to attract Little Jim's attention. At the sound of the handcuffs and the guard's words Little Jim sprang back against the wall. His eyes blazed. The guard slammed the door. "You aint gitten out without them," he threatened.

Little Jim pressed himself against the wall and crouched. His breathing was hard.

The guard stepped back. "Joe, go down and git Henry and Mack. And tell them to bring their forty-fours, loaded."

"You mustn't put those on him. Never!" Harriet cried.

"But—"

"He'll go without handcuffs. Ask him. *Ask* him."

"But what about that hoss out there? And it rearing wild all morning?"

"Ask him," she cried again.

The guard looked through the bars. "Will you go then, without the handcuffs?"

Jim's eyes were still blazing. The guard waited. Jim turned his eyes toward Harriet. Then he nodded.

In a few minutes the other guards came down the corridor. "Get your revolvers out," the guard ordered. He put the key again in the lock, but before he turned it he said to Harriet: "It's no place for a lady. If anything happened."

"I want to stay," she sobbed.

"Okay." Then to the guards. "Hold your guns ready."

However, the moment the door swung back, Little Jim moved into the corridor. He moved swiftly down. The guards tried to keep two at his side, the others behind, but the boy moved so swiftly they found themselves not guarding but hurrying, half-running, after him.

Harriet watched him disappear down the corridor, suddenly knowing that something of her was going with him, something half-real, like the terrible cry in her heart, like the strangeness of a far mountain place, when she could only touch the petal of the yellow trillium, not hold it, or even possess it, just know that it had been there for her.

Long before nine o'clock the courtroom had been crowded to the walls. By great maneuvering Thag Totten and Til Umbarger managed to keep places for Lennert and Dave Crockett. The room was tense. There were whispers that the jury in the last hours had had a turbulent time. Angry voices had been heard through the door of the jury room. No one knew for sure, but there were whisperings that Judge Spicer had sent word to them to come to some decision, or to report their inability to do so. But no one knew for a certainty.

Promptly at nine o'clock the sergeant-at-arms called the court to order. Judge Spicer came in from the rear door and took his place behind the bench.

The jury filed in. A hush fell over the room. Minutes passed. More minutes. The crowd began to move restlessly.

Judge Spicer looked at the leader of the jury. The clock ticked the seconds off. Prescott in his corner got up and began pacing nervously about his chair.

Someone brought a message to Richard Todd. He frowned. He got up and went up to Judge Spicer and talked to him in a low voice. Judge Spicer's face remained impassive. Richard Todd returned to his seat. There was a pallor in his cheeks and he was obviously forcing himself to show an outer calm. He took up a pencil and held it in his hands, the lead end in the fingers of one hand, the rubber end in the other.

Ten minutes passed.

And then down the corridor back of the judge's bench the crowd knew that Little Jim was coming. Necks craned. Breathing stopped. The boy came swiftly into the room, the guards crowding breathlessly behind him, their revolvers drawn. With no more than a pause he stepped up on the witness platform. There was a strange calmness in his way of doing it, and a great dignity. He stood straight, calm, and his very calmness made him tower above the room, above the nervous Prescott, the silent jury, the breathless crowd. His hands hung loosely down. His eyes looked straight ahead. If he saw anything, no one could tell. It was as if he were beyond anything the court or the crowd or the law could do to him.

Judge Spicer cleared his throat. "Does the jury find the prisoner guilty or not guilty?" His voice was clear and impersonal.

The leader of the jury stood up. "Your Honor," he said, "even after forty-eight hours the jury is still divided."

The pencil in Richard Todd's hands snapped.

"Does the leader of the jury feel that a decision can ever be reached by this jury based upon the evidence so far presented in this court?" Judge Spicer asked in the same even tone.

"No."

For a moment there was a stunned silence, and then as the meaning of the leader's word became clear, Til Umbarger sprang from his seat, shouting in rising excitement: "Who said the law could tech the Little Squire? Who said the law could tech the Little Squire?" And in the wave of Til's excitement an upward surge of emotion seized the room. Lucy McVay's lusty voice rose above the turmoil, "Hit's the Big Squire turnin in his grave and shakin the mountains. Hit's the Big Squire turnin in his grave."

Before Judge Spicer could stem the excitement, Little Jim himself was at his bench, striking it with his fist and crying: "Put me in that room. I'm not afeared of killed. Put me in that room, I tell you. A Boyden's not afeared of killed."

"Hit's the Big Squire turnin in his grave and shakin the mountains," Lucy's voice rose again in ecstasy.

Judge Spicer was on his feet, his face flushed in anger. The guards with one impulse rushed at Little Jim. One of them was thrown back. Instantly the others closed in about him, grasping his head, his shoulder, his legs. "Take your hands off me. Take your hands off me." His voice rose to an angry roar, flooding the room, ringing through the windows.

"The law caint tech the Little Squire! Who said the law could tech Little Squire?" Til cried again.

Then suddenly from outside, across the street, came an answering whinny, strident and wild. And following close upon the wild scream came the voices of men: "Hit's breakin loose. Hit's breakin loose. Look out. He's rearin. Ketch his head. Git out of his way. He'll kill you." Hoofs sounded on the pavement of the street. Then a heavy thud of hoofs landing on the Courthouse lawn. A wild clatter of hoofs on the Courthouse steps. On the marble porch. Another piercing scream. Those in the courtroom caught their breath in terror.

The attendant at the courtroom doors slammed them shut. For a moment the wild sounds from below were dulled. Then they became more terrifying. The sound of a violent scuffling in the vestibule below, shaking the walls, and frantic cries. "Git away from his teeth. Pull Sam from under the hoofs. Pull him." A cry of human agony cut through the clamor.

A revolver shot rang out. An agonized whinny, like a stricken scream, cut through the clamor. A louder confusion of hoofs, a clawing of walls. Then a heavy fall.

Two more shots.

The pendulum of the clock on the rear wall clicked three times in the silence. Judge Spicer held his gavel aloft. His eyes burned.

The pendulum clicked ten steady strokes.

"The sergeant-at-arms will open the door and ascertain the cause for this unnatural interruption of the court's procedure," Judge Spicer ordered. His voice was firm and biting.

The sergeant-at-arms opened the doors. He went into the hall and looked over the railing into the vestibule below. He came back to the door.

"It's all over," he said briefly.

"The guards will bring the prisoner before the bench," Judge Spicer ordered.

In the confusion and clamor from downstairs those in the courtroom had forgotten the guards who held Little

226

Jim smothered beneath them. The guards began disentangling themselves. One of them had covered Jim's head with a coat to muffle his cries. Jim stood up, but to the amazement of the guards he no longer struggled.

"The guards will stand free of the prisoner," Judge Spicer ordered.

The guards dropped their arms and stood back.

In the moment that they stood back, Little Jim moved swiftly through the rail gate. Down the aisle. Not a single hand stayed his going. The eyes of all followed him to the door. To those watching him it seemed only a moment, the click of a single stroke of the pendulum of the clock on the wall, that it took for him to pass down the aisle and disappear through the doors.

"Court is in recess," Judge Spicer intoned, striking the desk with his gavel.

Dazed, those in the courtroom stood up. They moved impulsively toward the door through which Little Jim had passed. Confusedly they crowded onto the balcony and down the steps that encircled the lower vestibule. They craned over the railing. In the pit below they saw Eldo lying sprawled, with Little Jim on the floor at the stallion's head, his arm along it and his own head so low that his hair mingled with the tangled mane. Outside, under the trees, the bay horse had always looked immense; but now, caught in the lower hall space between the double stairs, its head pulled awry, its great body flattened out—a great mass of flesh and hair and bone within the circle of eyes up and down the steps about its body—it looked even more enormous. Along its neck, where waves of light shaded off into the darker hair of the chest, was a trickle of blood. Over one eye was a blood-ringed bullet hole. Under the ear another.

A man near the stallion lifted his boot. He placed it on the stallion's haunch, as if to shove the weight; but the weight was too great, and the boot only succeeded in making the inert mass of flesh give slightly. The man had not time to withdraw his foot before an elbow next to him was raised. The elbow dug into the pit of his stomach.

"Keep yore God-damned foot off that hoss."

The man fell back into the crowd, coughing and holding his ribs.

"You ought've killed him, Thag."

A policeman moved in. He ordered those at the doors and on the steps to move on.

When the steps and the balcony and the courtroom were cleared, the policeman turned to Dave Crockett and Thag Totten.

"We're his folks," said Dave.

The policeman glanced at the bowed figure over the stallion's head. He nodded to Dave and went out.

THE YELLOW
TRILLIUM

    All afternoon Little Jim sat on the floor in the vestibule, his arm about the head of the stallion. No one went near him to disturb him. The Cove folk stood guard, outside and on the upper level of the balcony.

    The afternoon heat grew less. The guards changed. The night fell over the Courthouse. In time the lights in the stores and houses on the streets went out. The moon rose high over the trees, then waned. A faint breeze sprang up and rustled the leaves. Near four o'clock, when a faint white line was showing in the east over the rim of the distant mountain, a wagon with three horses, one in front of the other two, lumbered around the Courthouse to the front steps. Dave Crockett went up the steps into the vestibule. He could just discern the outline of the boy and the horse. If Little Jim had moved a muscle since morning Dave Crockett could not have told.

"Little Squire," Dave said, "hit's time to go back up to the Valley."

The boy did not stir.

"Little Jim," Dave began again, "we've brought a wagon to take Eldo back up to the Valley."

Little Jim moved from the horse's head and stood up.

Dave gave the signal to the others outside. They came in. With difficulty they began moving the horse out to the wagon. When finally they had it in the wagonbed, Dave said, "Little Squire, you git up in there and hold his head." Obediently Little Jim climbed into the wagon, and sitting on its floor took the horse's head onto his lap.

The wagon went around the Courthouse and into the street at the back, then around the Square to Main Street. There were four to ride on horseback in front, and more to ride behind. The procession moved toward the outskirts of Tateboro. Only a few early risers were awake to see the cortege go through.

The wagon moved on toward the Cove, through the foothills, and then up the winding mountain road, over the pass, and then down the long curving way until it reached the two boulders. It turned in.

When the wagon finally reached Little Stepper House,

the driver turned it on up the incline toward the Boyden graveyard, and halted it near a great mound of red dirt. Men with shovels were waiting.

"We figured you'd want him close to yore folks," Dave said to Jim. "You stand over there under that tree. We'll do the needful."

Little Jim climbed out of the wagon.

The men lowered the horse into the ground. Then they began with their shovels. They worked silently. Not one of them dared to look up. It was as if no one of them could bear to know what might be in the boy's face.

When the last shovel of dirt was on the mound, they turned to the tree. Little Jim was gone.

They looked at each other uneasily.

"Thag and me'll stay and speak to the Little Squire when he comes to the house," Dave said.

After all had gone Dave said, "I reckon we'd best wait close to the house."

The sun was high. A locust in a nearby tree sent forth its song of late summer: "Six weeks to frost . . . six weeks to frost . . . to frost. . . ."

Near five o'clock the leaves rustled in a cooling breeze. The shadows grew long. The sun sank behind Hanging Rock.

Finally Thag said, "Maybe he's waitin fer jest the one of us."

Dave made no answer.

Thag stood up. "I'll stop by and tell Martha you're waitin to speak to him," he said. He paused. "Tell the Little Squire—" He looked back toward the trees above the incline leading to the graveyard. He shook his head. "I

231

reckon he'll know without the sayin of the words." He strode off down the lane. Dave waited alone.

The distant trees grew gray in the twilight; then black. Dave sighed. Finally, when the tip of a full moon showed above the trees, Dave stood up and went toward the kitchen. From under a stone near the door he took a heavy brass key. He had hidden it there the day they had come to take Little Jim into Tateboro. He put the key in the kitchen lock and turned it. He pushed open the door. Striking a match, he found a candle and, lighting it, placed it in a saucer on the table. The faint light lit up the room. The kitchen was much as he remembered it when, a very long time before it seemed to him, he had accompanied Father O'Brian into the Valley the night Amelia Boyden died.

He sat down near the fireplace. A field mouse scurried across the floor.

The candle burned lower. Finally Dave stood up. "Martha'll be uneasy," he muttered. He looked at the candle. "I'll jest leave the candle burnin."

Setting the door slightly ajar, with the key in it, he went outside. He didn't want to go. Perhaps a little while longer. He hesitated. Then he thought of the tree up there near the graveyard. Maybe the boy was waiting there.

He climbed the hill. The moon high in the sky etched in silver the outlines of the trees and the tilted gravestones. He went close to the tree under which he had told Little Jim to stand. Little Jim was not there.

He shook his head. "Maybe he'll come out to the mill when he sets his mind to it," Dave murmured. He turned down the hill, and, following the road now clear in the moonlight, started out of the Valley.

The next day Old Dave puttered around his office and near the porch so that he would be close by if the boy came; but Little Jim did not come that day, or the next. A week passed, and another, and still another. The leaves along the road in front of his mill turned from green to red-and-gold, and then the November winds sprang up and blew them brown among the rocks. And still Little Jim did not come to the mill. As the December days grew colder, Dave found every excuse to lift the lever and stop the water over the great wheel so that he might go out to the porch to look down the road.

A light snow fell in January. The February ice turned into March thaws. Martha tried to comfort him. "I was talkin to Annie Umbarger today. She says the Little Squire never was one to come out of the Valley till spring time, lessen it suited him."

"But the Little Squire were always one to come," Dave lamented. He looked at the silver goblets in the corner cupboard. "Hit weren't more'n a week, when his maw died."

"Jest wait," Martha urged. "Jest you wait."

In April Annie pulled back the leaves from the earth behind her hawthorn bush. Her sharp eyes saw a crack in the earth, and deep inside it was a pale-green shoot. Excitedly she ran into her house, crying, "He's fetched it back! He's fetched it back!"

Til looked up in surprise.

"Come out and look. Come out and look." And she took him to the hawthorn. "Little Squire's fetched my yeller trillie back."

Til looked close to the ground. He searched along the fence. "I don't see any tracks."

"But he'd fetched it a long way back. Hit's been in the ground and growin. You'll be seein tracks in my yard come bloomin time fer my trillies." Her eyes were bright.

"But how you know that'n aint jest a shoot-off root from the one he took?" Til asked uneasily.

Annie turned from him. "I'm not tellin you anything more, Til, ef that's the way you're goin to take it."

Til got down on his knees and looked more closely. "When do you reckon he brought it back?"

"In the night time," she whispered, "when we was asleep. And when the dawg-star begins to set over Old Hangin Rock, you'll see his tracks leadin to the Rock. Mark my words. And in the day time he'll be settin there under my lilac trees, bitin my lily-blooms."

But in April Annie's white trillium and red trillium grew tall and fell into seed; behind the hawthorn bush the single yellow trillium grew tall, and it too fell into seed; yet Little Jim did not come to lie in the shade of her lilac tree or to sit on the fence and throw his shadow across her May violets.

But one night in June when the rains fell with the violence of a cloudburst and the lightning cut across the Valley in blinding flame and the thunder rolled across the

mountaintops with such a roar that the Cove folk thought
Hanging Rock would surely fall, Til stumbled down Sleeping Father Mountain. He was drenched to the skin and
his teeth were chattering. "I saw the Little Squire on the
Rock. I seed him clear in the night, standin there, and the
ground shakin under my feet from the thunder."

"And what else did you see?" Annie cried.

"I saw a hoss."

"A hoss?"

Til nodded, his eyes burning.

"What color were his hoss?"

"Red. Redder'n the Big Squire's hair in the sun."

"I knowed it," Annie breathed. "I knowed it."

But when Til told Thag Totten of what he had seen,
Thag scowled. "I never heared him passin my house."

"Hit were thunderin."

"But I never seed his hoss tracks in my fields."

"Maybe he aint ridin by yore house to git there," Til
answered.

"Maybe," answered Thag.

"He fetched Annie's flower back in the winter time and
he left no tracks."

Thag looked at Til with narrowed eyes. "What flower?"

"Hern."

Thag shifted.

"I reckon he always did have more of a leanin toward
Annie than to most folks," Til defended. "And he knows
of the sweet lovin in her heart fer him."

Thag scowled. "He's welcome to make his tracks acrost
my land any day or night time," he answered sharply.

The summer passed and the November frosts nipped the October leaves again, and the late February winds blew the snow over the thin ice of Dave Crockett's mill pond, yet no one could say they had seen Little Jim at the Cove or near the Cove. Over a year and a half had passed. A deep, inexpressible uneasiness lay about their hearts.

One night in early March Til said to Annie, "Dave Crockett let on to me today that he wants me to ride in to the Valley to speak to the Little Squire."

"Little Squire never invited pryin into his ways."

"Dave allowed that long as he come in yore garden to fetch yore flower . . . Dave Crockett wants me to go," Til went on doggedly. "And I'm aimed to do what Dave Crockett wants."

"Well, it's not to my likin," she insisted.

"I'm jest takin a word to him from Dave Crockett," Til answered.

The next morning, however, when Til woke up he found that Annie had been up long before him.

"Jest bakin a pan of sweet cakes fer you to take to the Little Squire," she said, "as long as you're goin."

When Til on his mule went through the entrance of the Valley, the sun was just over the far side of Little Stepper Mountain; but when he rode up to Little Stepper House, it was high above the trees. The house looked cold and windswept, and except for the open windows of the upper room, had a curious air of vacancy about it. Til glanced up to the windows. He thought of calling out, but decided it would be better to go around to the back. He tied his mule to a tree and went to the kitchen door. The

236

door was open. "I'm comin by to say howdy, Little Squire," he called out. "I brought a word from Dave Crockett."

He waited a moment, and then knocked. There was no answer. He peered in the doorway. Withered leaves were on the floor and table, as if blown there through the open door. Signs of seepage of rain too were on the floor. Uneasily Til stepped inside. "Howdy, Little Squire," he called again. There was a stirring in the room back of the kitchen. Then a sound of claws on the floor. A fox ran into the kitchen and out the door. The leaves on the floor rattled under its swift feet. From a nest in the rafter over the mantel a bird flew over his head and out the door.

"Reckon he don't live in this part of the house no more," Til said aloud. "But I've come this fer, and maybe he's up there in that room and jest don't hear me."

He went into the hall. Stray leaves from the kitchen crunched under his feet. "Howdy, Little Squire," he called, loud enough to be heard ahead of him. He climbed the stairs and, going to the door of the corner room with the open windows, he shouted, "I've brought a word from Dave Crockett." He knocked hard on the door. It swung slightly ajar. Til pushed it open slowly. A few dried leaves moved back with it, making a slight scraping sound. The windows on the far side were wide-open. Two beds were in the room. Only one was empty.

The roots of Til's hair crawled and caught themselves into knots on his scalp. For a moment he could not move. Then he fell back and blindly stumbled down the stairs. He staggered out of the kitchen. He ran to his mule and tried to untie the halter, but his hands were shaking so that

237

he could hardly get the knot unfastened. The mule, sensing his terror, reared. Til struggled to hold it. He clambered into the saddle and turned down the lane.

When Til pulled up in front of Dave Crockett's mill he was breathless. "Dave Crockett. Dave Crockett," he cried, running into the mill. "Hit's the Little Squire. The Little Squire."

Dave came hurrying. "Did you see him?"

"Yes. But not the way you're thinkin. He's layin up there in his bed."

"Sick?"

Til's hands moved wildly. "He's past bein sick. He aint been livin a long time. He don't look like hisself." And he put his hand up to his eyes as if he would shut out the thing he had seen.

"Ride over to Thag Totten's," Dave said, "and take my hoss while yore mule rests."

When Til was in the saddle Dave said: "Don't say a word to nobody but Thag Totten. Maybe you've not seen what you think you've seen."

Til did not wait to reply.

Near two o'clock the three men drew up at the rear of Little Stepper House.

"In that room up there with the winders open," Til pointed. "But I'm stayin down here in the yard with the hosses. I'm never goin up in that room again."

Thag and Dave went in.

After a time they came down. They were pale and shaken.

"Hit were the Little Squire?" Til asked.

Thag nodded.

"Reckon you ken do one more trip, Til?" Dave asked, his voice trembling. "Ken you ride to the mill to tell Martha I won't be home fer the night? And I reckon," he hesitated, "you'll have to let Annie and the folks know."

Dave turned to Thag. "And before folks start comin we'll have to git some boards and nails."

"I'll bring Annie back to help with the layin out," Til said, riding off.

Soon after dark Annie arrived at Little Stepper House. She had walked the distance alone. Dave met her in the kitchen door. "Til's takin the news around," she said, removing her bonnet. "I come as fast as I could."

"We just moved Little Squire into the big room," Dave said, leading her into the hall. The sound of a pounding hammer reverberated through the walls. A single candle burned in the room. Between two chairs Annie saw the rude coffin. Thag, hammer in hand, looked up. "Thag's jest puttin in the last nails," Dave said.

Annie put her hand out to steady herself. She shook her head as if she could not understand. "But I come almost runnin to help with the layin out," she said, her voice unsteady.

"Dave and me have done all the layin out anybody'll ever do fer the Little Squire," Thag answered.

"But I come to do the layin out," Annie repeated, as if Thag's words had not been uttered.

"Hit were not a thing fer a woman to do, and her with too much lovin in the heart," Dave answered. "Hit near tore the heart out of me to see him layin up there."

Annie leaned against the doorway for a moment, her

eyes searching Dave's face. Then she turned abruptly and left the two men.

"Hit's no way fer a woman to act, and the Little Squire a-layin close by in a coffin," Thag muttered.

"Maybe I'd better explain to her more," Dave mumbled. Dave found Annie in the kitchen. "Annie," he began.

But Annie would not notice him. She moved busily about the room, mumbling to herself, "All my days and all my nights I waited to help at the buryin of the Big Squire—"

"But that were the doins of Old Lady Boyden, not ourn," Dave tried to interrupt.

"And now the likes of a Totten—"

"But Annie—"

"All my days and nights—"

"Annie," Dave insisted; "hit were to save you we did fer him."

Annie paused only a second to ask, "Were he lyin up there in that room with the winders open, like Til said?"

"Yes."

"Then ef you don't need old Annie's help, you don't need her thinkin."

"But it were fer—"

But she would not talk with him further. She was at the fireplace and lighting a taper. She carried the flame to the corner and touched it to a candle in the rose cup under the crucifix. "Fer the Little Squire," she murmured. "Miss Harriet always said he kept a candle burnin, and I'm aimed to light it fer him till he comes back."

"But Annie . . ."

"The Little Squire had his way of thinkin."

Dave sighed in relief. "I been worryin what you'd think when I said I were goin to send fer his kind of preacher."

"You men folks run this to suit yoreselves," she answered doggedly. "Taint fer Annie to add her say."

"But you . . ." and he pointed to the candle.

"I'd do most anything fer the Little Squire," she answered. She had found a broom and, lifting it, went on talking. "Folks'll be troopin in before daylight. This kitchen needs sweepin. I'm fixin up fer the Little Squire. He's always needed a woman."

Dave retreated, shaking his head stupidly. "Annie don't act right in the head," he muttered to Thag. "Maybe we—"

By noon the next day the whole mountainside seemed to have converged in Little Stepper Valley, and at sundown they laid pallets in the outhouses and on the porches to sleep the night. All afternoon they had filed through the long room to stare at the coffin. Thag Totten and Dave were watchful that only those who had been close to the Little Squire were allowed to stay long in the house. Guards were stationed in the doorway of the drawing room to keep vigil. Annie had lit a kerosene lamp and taken it into the room and set it on a table near the coffin. "No candles are gonna burn in this room," she said. No one dared argue with her.

The light made a dim fringe on the portraits on the walls, over the dusty brocades and crystal, and over the two watchers in their vigil beside the door. She backed awkwardly out of the room.

Sometime in the night Dave climbed the stairs. He remembered the way Little Jim had told him to go that night in the jail. He went down the hall. He opened the door of the room at the end of the hall. With difficulty he moved the bed from the wall of the room. Another door was behind it. In the next room he found the chests piled one on the other. They were heavy to move, but it was his to do, and only his. Finally he found the table under the pile of quilts and curtains. Carefully he brought it downstairs. When he reached the lower floor he did not know what to do with it. But Little Jim had asked him to get it. He turned into the long room. He carried the table to a place close to the coffin. Jim would want it there. Then he went back into the kitchen.

Throughout the night the watch changed every two hours. In the kitchen the women brewed hot drinks in the big fireplace and talked quietly with the men as they came in out of the night to take their turns. The high March winds whistled around the chimneys, sometimes making the flames dance awkwardly and bulge puffs of smoke into the room.

In a corner beside the mantel, as far away from the lighted candle under the crucifix as he could get, Thag Totten sat, a shadow on his face. From time to time he looked at the flickering light, shaded by its cup, and then he would uncross and cross his legs uneasily. Annie Umbarger, watching his movements, read his thoughts. "I lighted that candle with my own hands," she said, "fer the Little Squire."

Thag made no answer.

Late in the night someone found a soiled book. Its corners were gnawed by little foxes' teeth. The finder read the title aloud slowly: *A Young Reader's Robinson*

Crusoe. He opened the cover and read aloud the inscription: 'To James Braxton Boyden from Harriet Evans.' He turned the finger-worn pages. He passed the book around.

When the book came to Maybelle Shelton, she looked at the pages and then said suddenly, "I'm aimed to keep this book myself."

Clonda Hollister looked up. "Ef the Little Squire had a-wanted you to have it, he'd a-give it to you."

"But I want it fer little Ludy to read nights when he gits old enough," Maybelle insisted.

"Ef it comes to that, they's two or three others got a right to it," Clonda answered. "Besides it were Miss Harriet give that to the Little Squire."

Maybelle flushed. The folk in the kitchen rustled in their chairs.

"Maybe it's fer jest the Little Squire to keep, Maybelle," Annie added quietly. "When he comes back."

Thag got up abruptly and went outside. After a time Old Dave followed him. He found Thag sitting on a log on a rise of ground away from the buildings. The sky was bright with stars, and the rims of Little Stepper and Longer Stepper mountains in the distance made a heavy mass against the luminous heavens. Old Dave sat down beside Thag. After a time Thag said, "Annie don't seem natural about the Little Squire."

Old Dave shook his head sadly. "I reckon taint fer us men folks to know the way of a lovin heart of a woman fer a boy, when she aint got one of her own."

"Hit's more'n that. She lit the candle with her own hands."

"Yes. But it were me that sent fer his kind of preacher fer the buryin."

"I weren't with you on that, Dave Crockett. And Annie were against you, too. And then she lit the candle."

"I know. But it's Little Squire's way of thinkin, not ourn. And ef the Old Lady's will holds, the Catholics'll git the land anyhow."

"That's what's gnawin at me too, night an day," Thag burst out. "The Catholics gitten up here in these mountains, ownin lands and lightin candles an doin harm."

"I reckon it's all the same, Thag Totten," Old Dave answered quietly, "as long as God's gitten it to do with."

"God's no Catholic! God's a Foot-washin Baptist. And a Democrat besides."

Old Dave did not answer. For a long time neither spoke. Finally Dave broke the silence. "The Old Lady Boyden never done me harm, Thag." He paused. Thag did not answer. The silence was long. Then Dave went on, "She set great store by some things I aint able to see." Thag said nothing. "And you, Thag Totten," he continued, looking off into the dark trees, "you set great store by another way of doin, foot-washin and baptizin and shoutin and singin. I don't. But I never fretted. And here we two sit, in the night time, talkin, and no hard feelins." He let his hands rest on his knees. "And there's Annie Umbarger. She believes she ken stop blood by jest readin out the Bible. Seems like she does it, too, more times than not."

He paused. Still Thag said nothing.

"Like runnin my mill," Old Dave went on. "I go in there, open up them sluice gates, and wheels start turnin.

244

I pour in some corn, and after a while meal comes out. Hit's the way my daddy did before me, and his daddy before him. But come a time I won't be a-doin it, maybe somebody else'll be liftin the sluice gates. Or gitten in a new way of turnin the wheel, or maybe even a new wheel. And what'll come out'll seem different, to some folks. But somehow the doin won't be much different, I reckon, and what'll be comin out won't be much different. A man jest has to do what comes his way, I reckon, the best he knows."

Old Dave stopped. A falling star, flashing swiftly in the heavens, burned bright, then disappeared behind the rim of Little Stepper Mountain.

"I'm follerin yore words, Dave Crockett," Thag said.

Dave roused himself. "They's a whole world of folks over there," and he pointed beyond the mountains, "doin some way which is special to them. Not my way maybe. But I don't mind the things that's done different, ef they don't mean harm to folks. But the one thing that hurts so deep I caint hardly stir, hurts so I caint figure it out, and that's . . ." He rubbed his chin with the back of his hand. "And that's a boy what's—" the word stuck in his throat and he could only murmur almost inaudibly, "before he had his chance."

The next morning near eleven Father O'Brian arrived on horseback. Old Dave went out to meet him. Father O'Brian came into the house and spoke quietly to those near him. They took him into the long drawing room. The lamp was still burning. The watchers stood up. He performed the last rites, and when he had finished he gave the signal, and they lifted the box and moved out of the house up to the graveyard.

The folk were already there. No one had ever seen so many together in all the years. Father O'Brian at the head of the grave read the service, intoning the Latin with simplicity. Then he paused and looked at Old Dave, who stood at the foot of the grave.

The wild March winds rode high. Those on the outside turned uneasily toward the hedge, half-expecting a sudden grind of wheels, a clatter of hoofs, and the carriage of Old Lady Gwynn to break through. Only dry leaves shifted in the wind.

Old Dave, his white hair bare, finally began. His voice was low and gentle. "I knowed him since he was a little thing, and all along. Little Squire always did to suit hisself. Taint right to say he didn't." He looked slowly into the eyes of those about him. "But no man, livin nor dead, ken rightly say Little Squire ever meant to do him harm." He raised his hand slowly in a gesture of profound benediction. Father O'Brian lifted a handful of red clay and held it over the grave. *"Memento homo quia est et pulvem reveritas,"* he intoned. The red clay fell upon the box.

Gradually the crowd began to break away.

Those with shovels filled in the hole and made a red mound. Then they brought two pieces of gray sandstone. One of them had already been chiseled. It bore the name of the Big Squire and the date of his death. 'Killed' was cut deep into the stone. They placed it at the place where they remembered his mound.

"Hit aint fitten," Lou Campbell argued, "fer the Old Lady to die and never set a stone to his head."

"Reckon hit were jest her way," Will Hollister answered.

The other piece of stone was unfinished. But Til Umbarger had chalked in the inscription. Ollie Montgomerie, holding the chisel and mallet in hand, read the chalked lettering to himself, and then asked in a troubled voice, "You aimin to have me cut 'Killed' on here, even ef he did jest die in a bed?"

Old Dave turned around. "One way you look at, he might've died," he said slowly. "And then, another way, I reckon he were killed, that day at the court-trial." And he looked toward the mound near the tree that they had made the day when they brought Little Jim and his horse back to the Valley.

"But I aint aimin to say somethin not exactly right on a tombstone," argued Ollie.

"Jest read what's on some stones I've seed, and recollect how what's under the writin were afore they died," Til answered.

"Somethin in that," agreed Alan Holt, standing beside Til. "And it air a shame to ruin a record. Look at them other stones over there. 'Killed.' And that'n—'Killed.' And that'n—'Killed.' And that'n—"

"But—"

"Hit aint gonna do no harm," Til persisted, anger in his eyes, "to take a chance. Little Squire Jim'd a-been killed, natural, ef he'd jest had the time."

"That's a fact," Alan took up the argument. "And them that wants ken say, readin it, 'But he wont killed. Nobody

247

give him time to git killed.' Hit can go by word of mouth. Aint that right, Thag?" Alan turned toward Thag Totten.

"I vote fer 'Killed,' " said Thag tersely.

Ollie still held the mallet and chisel poised. "All I say is, hit's agin my nature—"

"Ef you don't want to do the cuttin, give me the things. I'll do it," Til flared.

"No." And Ollie drew the tools back as if he feared Til would take them from him by force. "I've counted a long time on cuttin Little Squire Jim's tombstone. And I'm aimed to do it."

"Then do it, and quit arguin," said Til.

Til stood over him belligerently while with the chisel Ollie dug the letters out carefully: 'James Braxton Boyden.' He stopped and looked up, his eyes pained.

"Go on," said Til.

Ollie again bent over the sandstone. Slowly he cut a *K*, then an *i* and an *l* into the stone. When he was safely into the second *l*, Thag Totten left him and walked along the hill with Dave Crockett. They stopped near the house, looking about them—at the rolling hills of the Valley, the thick forests that swept up to the crests of Little Stepper and Big Stepper mountains, at the log outhouses, once slave-tended, the chimneys and thick walls of Little Stepper House.

"I still don't hold with them Catholics gitten up in these mountains."

"I reckon it's what them that owned it wanted," Old Dave answered.

By late afternoon nearly all the folk had gone. Old Dave and Thag Totten waited under a tree while Annie Umbarger finished talking to Father O'Brian. The priest was near the kitchen door. Though talking to him, Annie had not gone too close. Til hovered protectively at her back.

"Ef it's not askin too much," Annie was saying bravely, "I'd be wonderin ef you'd let me borrow somethin out of that there house."

"What would you wish?" Father O'Brian asked kindly.

Annie hesitated. Then, "Little Squire borrowed somethin of mine, and it pleasured me no end, and . . ." she faltered.

"And you wish to borrow something of his?"

She nodded.

"What is it?"

Annie searched the face of the priest. "In the spring and summer time I won't be needin nothin," she finally said. "I'll be fixin my flowers, and I'm liable to look most anytime and see Little Jim a-settin somers around, like he used to. Under my lilac tree, maybe, or eatin my trillies, ef he likes." She paused uncertainly, and then rushed on. "But in the winter time, when things are brown and hid in the dirt—I'm wonderin ef I could jest have the keepin of that candle and red thing to hold it, and that—"

"The crucifix?"

Annie nodded.

Father O'Brian turned and went into the house and brought the crucifix and rose candle-cup. He placed them in her hands.

"I'm proud to be beholden to you," she murmured. She

249

backed away. Then she stopped. Something in the priest's face made her add:

"I'm not takin it fer good. Hit's the Little Squire's, jest like always. But he always seem to set great store by it. And come some dark night, when the winds is ridin high, and the rain and lightnin is slashin about, I'm aimed to keep it lighted. And when Little Squire comes gallopin by, wild and rearin, he'll see it shinin through my winder. And then I aint gonna be fazed one minute ef he comes ridin that hoss of hissen right into the room, them eyes of hissen burnin black the way they do when he gits stirred up, and him a-sayin, 'Who give you my candle burnin in the winder?' And I'm aimed to say, 'Git off yore hoss, Little Squire, an draw up a cheer.' And when he do it, I'm aimed to ask him somethin."

"What you aimin to ask him?" Til interrupted.

A glint of a smile came into Annie's eyes. "I'm not tellin everything I'm thinkin. Hit'll jest be between the Little Squire and me."

Father O'Brian looked at her with a keen glance. "And after the Little Squire's had his visit with you, would you tell him to be sure and come by and see me too?"

Annie bobbed her head. "But I'm aimed to keep him as long as I ken a-settin in my own chair."

Father O'Brian smiled again, but his eyes still searched her face.

When Annie was down the road Old Dave came up and shook hands with the priest, and then rejoined Thag. Together they went down the road. They walked on in silence.

250

That night Annie and Til sat in front of their hearth. Til smoked his pipe thoughtfully. Outside the wind rode high, dipping now and then to swirl around the chimney. The fire flared, sending up a bright glow, then dimmed.

Annie, her fingers working nimbly with herbs, rocked back and forth, the tips of her shoes lightly keeping the chair in motion. From time to time she turned to look at the candle burning in its cup in the window. Its flame gave to the whole window an aura of rose light. Suddenly she heard from the outside the stroke of a hoof on the stone path, and a voice calling out "Howdy."

"Hit's Thag Totten's voice," said Til in surprise, "and it this time of night." He got up and unbarred the door. "Come in, Thag Totten. Draw up a cheer and set."

Thag came inside, but to Til's invitation to take a seat he shook his head. He glanced toward the candle in the window. He shifted uneasily. Finally he said, "Hit's on my mind, and I had to come."

"What's on yore mind, Thag Totten?" Annie asked, still busy with her herbs.

Thag looked again at the candle in the window. "Hit's the burnin of that candle in yore house, and bringin that thing home."

"Hit's my winder, Thag Totten," Annie answered in even voice.

"I'm not arguin that," Thag went on. "But I'm not wantin harm to come yore way. Since the time you helped me with little Maybelle, what's harm to you is harm to me."

Annie stopped her rocking. "I'm much obliged fer the

feelin, Thag Totten," she said, "but hit's my winder."
Then, softening at the thought of the meaning of his
words, she added, "I'm jest burnin it till the Little Squire
comes ridin by to take it back."

"That don't make a grain of sense, Annie," Thag interrupted.

"Hit makes sense to me," Annie answered.

"But how's the Little Squire goin to come ridin by when
he's layin up there in the ground this minute with 'Killed'
wrote on his tombstone?"

"Killed?"

"Yes. And Til, yore own husband, were there fer the
cuttin."

"One way of lookin at it," Annie answered slowly, "he
were killed that day . . . anyhow, a part of him folks always
knowed was. But how you know Little Squire's dead?"

"But aint you jest come back yoreself from the buryin
of the Little Squire?"

"Not me."

"But you was there. I saw you with my own eyes."

"I know, and you men folks runnin things to suit yoreselves." She held an herb up to the light, turning the leaf
over and over as if searching out some peculiar quality in
it. "How you know, Thag Totten," she asked, still examining the leaf as if the leaf were a very important thing in the
world, "that you've not been this day jest to the buryin of
the Big Squire?"

"What're you sayin, Annie Umbarger?" Thag burst out.
"The Big Squire's been killed and layin in his grave up
there more'n ten years."

"I never saw the Big Squire put in the ground," Annie

252

went on, still peering at the leaf with her sharp little eyes. "And I've never met a man or woman that were there to see the Big Squire put in the ground."

"But—"

"Then," and she turned to look at him directly, "how you know you an Dave Crockett aint in the last day or two jest laid out the Big Squire and helped to put him in his grave?"

"But it'd not be natural, and him killed these ten years."

"Nothin ever happened in that valley ever been natural to some folks. The Old Lady Boyden weren't natural. But she had a great lovin fer the Big Squire, and I'd not set it above her way of thinkin and lovin to try to keep him in her way, ef it suited her. And more'n that, ef you ever knowed which way the Little Squire were gonna do, or was thinkin, you're smarter'n I am, Thag Totten, and I'd never agree to that."

"But hit were the Little Squire that Dave Crockett and me put in that coffin," he answered doggedly.

"How'd you know hit were the Little Squire?" Annie shot back, still looking him straight in the eyes.

"Hit were Little Jim's red hair."

"The Big Squire had red hair," Annie countered.

"And he were the Little Squire's size. And his shirt. The one he wore to the court-trial."

"Didn't they find a shirt jest like it in Beldie Thomas' house? They were all the Big Squire's to begin with."

Thag turned to Til. "You were there, Til Umbarger. You saw him layin in the bed."

Til shifted. "I'm not takin sides with a Totten against Annie," he said.

Thag backed toward the door. "I'm not stayin in this house another minute. Lightin candles and talkin words straight from the Devil. But I tell you this, Annie Umbarger. I know what I've seen. Hit were the Little Squire I nailed in that box, an Dave Crockett were there to say so."

"Tell me, Thag Totten," Annie followed him to the door. "Did you see him that night when he rode by and cured little Maybelle?"

"No. But I heared him."

"But did you see him?"

"No."

"Then yore words don't make sense to me neither," she said.

When Thag was gone Annie went to the window. She rubbed her fingers over the rose bowl softly. "Til," she said, "I'm not askin you to take sides. You've always been a man to do yore own thinkin an doin. And I'm not askin you ef you've jest been to the buryin of the Big Squire after all this time."

Til puffed his pipe in silence.

Annie leaned against the window. She peered out into the darkness. "Hit's a high wind. Hit's a night fer the Little Squire, ef it suited him."

She paused, but when Til did not answer, she went on. "The Little Squire's never come out of the Valley lessen it suited him. But I'm thinkin an dreamin hit'll suit him to come ridin out when my trillies are in bloom, come the breathin of spring again."

"What were that question you're gonna ask him?" Til finally said.

Annie let her hand move in the candlelight, ever so gently. "I'm aimed to ask him what he do with my yeller trillie when he fetched it away in the spring time," she whispered softly.

"But he fetched it back," Til said.

"I know."

"The Little Squire never were one to invite pryin into his ways . . ."

Annie smiled. "I'll not be pryin," she murmured, "and I reckon I already know without the askin. But it'd pleasure me, and set my heart to healin, jest to see that boy look in his face again, and hear him jest not tellin me, when I ask him."